Scottie let out a ragged breath, trying to smile. "You're being too nice."

"Sorry, it's in my DNA. Nothing I can do about it," Bryce told her, leaning in closer as he wiped away another tear that insisted on spilling out.

The moment seemed to freeze, embossing itself on the folds of time. Very slowly, Bryce lowered his mouth to hers. It was a kiss meant to comfort, a kiss to tell her it was all right to cry. A kiss to let her know that she wasn't alone in this, that he was there for her and would continue to be there for her.

It bordered on more.

She knew she shouldn't have let it happen, or, at the very least, that she should have pulled back when it began. But once his lips touched hers, she realized that she was hungrier for comfort than she thought was humanly possible.

* * *

Be sure to check out the next books in this exciting series:

Cavanaugh Justice—Where Aurora's finest are always in action

CAVANAUGH ON CALL

BY
MARIE FERRARELLA

First Published in Great Britain 2017
By Mills & Boon, an imprint of HarperCollins*Publishers*
1 London Bridge Street, London, SE1 9GF

© 2017 Marie Rydzynski-Ferrarella

ISBN: 978-0-263-93039-9

18-0517

USA TODAY bestselling and RITA® Award-winning author **Marie Ferrarella** has written more than two-hundred-and-fifty books for Mills & Boon, some under the name Marie Nicole. Her romances are beloved by fans worldwide. Visit her website, www.marieferrarella.com.

Prologue

Alexandra Scott eased herself slowly into the closest chair at the kitchen table. Her eyes were still half closed even though she'd already showered, dressed and poured the obligatory mug of inky-black coffee that she needed to jump-start her day.

Holding the oversize mug with both hands, she forced herself to take a deep sip of the brew. It tasted like hot sludge. Scottie hated black coffee, but she wasn't drinking it for pleasure. She was drinking it because she had to. If she didn't, she was liable to wind up sleepwalking through half her day—if not more.

The strong, black liquid landed in the pit of her stomach, spreading out like an oil slick: thick and impenetrable. Slowly it flowed through her entire body, rousing everything in its path until the sum total of her was not only awake but keenly alert.

Setting down the mug, the homicide detective took a deep breath and then blew it out again. Her breath made the wayward strands of dark blond bangs move ever so slightly.

She pushed them back impatiently. She wasn't one who fussed with her hair, but it would be nice if it could stay put.

How was it that mornings kept arriving faster and faster these days? It felt as if she had just laid her head down on her pillow and here it was, time to get up again and face a full day.

There should be a law, Scottie thought as she reached for the paper she'd automatically picked up at her front door and brought in with her, that mornings weren't allowed to arrive until after a person had had six decent hours' sleep. After all, it wasn't as if she'd been out carousing, enjoying Aurora's limited nightlife. She'd been out keeping the citizens of that same city safe so that *they* could enjoy carousing or whatever it was that people enjoyed doing these days. She really wouldn't know about that. Working one job or another since before she'd turned eighteen, for the last few years she'd been a homicide detective and that had consumed almost all of her life.

Not that she minded, but it would be nice to get a good night's sleep every now and then.

Stifling a yawn, Scottie blinked once and tried to focus on the newspaper in front of her.

The local paper was her one attachment to her

past. While everyone she knew got their news in sound bites or from the internet, Scottie still preferred to get hers from newsprint. Her late grandfather, the man she'd been named after, had been a journalist and, in a way, though the man had died when she was seven, reading the newspaper—when she had the time for it—made her feel close to the man.

She missed those days. Missed not feeling as if the world was on her shoulders.

"C'mon, Scottie, drink up. Don't dawdle," she urged herself under her breath. "You'll be late for work and you don't want th—"

Scottie almost dropped the mug she'd raised to her lips. Moving like someone in a dream, she set the mug down, her eyes never leaving the story above the fold. The one she'd just fleetingly—and unconsciously—glanced at.

She'd had no intention of reading any of the stories on page one. She'd only meant to glance at a few words here and there in passing, drink the rest of the vile black brew and go. But something had just jumped out at her, commandeering her eyes and grabbing her full attention. When she thought about it later, she wouldn't have even been able to explain why. There was just something—*something*—about the story that forced her to sit up and actually absorb the words.

Scottie got no further than the first three lines of the first paragraph before the taste of bile rose in her throat and filled her mouth at the same time she felt the pit of her stomach sink, pinching the sides together.

No!

"No, no, no, no!" she cried out loud, her voice bordering on outrage. "This isn't happening. This has to be someone else. It *has* to be."

But even as she shouted the words at the news article on page one, Scottie had a sick feeling she wasn't being paranoid.

She was correct.

Ethan.

She had to call her brother and once she had him on the phone, he'd tell her she was wrong. Not in so many words, but by his tone, his inflection. By the unspoken hurt in his voice that she would even *think* he was involved. She'd known Ethan his entire life and she'd know if he was lying or trying to keep the truth from her.

Willing her hand not to tremble, Scottie hit the number on her cell that would connect her directly to Ethan's phone, all the while telling herself that this was just a coincidence. An awful, unsettling coincidence. She had worked much too hard to get him back to the straight and narrow and *he* had worked with her. He'd been clean and out of trouble for almost five years now. Five whole years.

He wouldn't do this.

Not to himself.

Not to her.

"This isn't you!" she fairly shouted at the newspaper as she listened to the phone on the other end ring.

On the sixth ring, Scottie snapped to attention. She heard Ethan's voice.

"This is Ethan Loomis. I'm not available right now. Please leave a message and your number and I'll get back to you."

Fear and anger had her throat suddenly so dry she could barely get the words out. "Ethan, this is Scottie. Call me. *Now!*"

When she terminated the call, Scottie picked up the newspaper and finished reading the article.

Her hands were shaking.

Chapter 1

"You've *got* to be kidding me."

Detective Bryce Cavanaugh watched in disbelief as his partner, Detective Peter Phelps, a tall, thin man whose suit jackets hung loosely off his body, packed the last of his personal items into a cardboard box. "You're actually *leaving*?" Bryce questioned.

"And they said you'd never amount to anything as a detective," Phelps said dryly, tossing a half-empty bag of stale chocolate-covered wafers from last Halloween into the box. "Yeah," the older man said more seriously. "You figured it out. I'm leaving."

"Was it something I said?" Bryce's voice cracked, trying to cover up the fact that if this was on the level, it left him far from happy and somewhat surprised. He wasn't averse to change, but he didn't exactly welcome a major shake-up, either.

"Hell, it's everything you said," Phelps answered tongue in cheek as he opened one drawer after another, checking for anything he might have left behind. "But if you're asking why I'm leaving the police department, you don't have anything to do with it."

Bryce took a seat on the edge of his partner's desk, crossing his arms before him. "Then educate me, Phelps. Why are you suddenly spring-cleaning your desk two months late?"

The frown on Phelps's long, gaunt face went clear to the bone. "Alice's mom is sick," he said, referring to his wife's only living parent.

Bryce knew enough to look immediately sympathetic. "Hey, I'm sorry to hear that." Still perched on the desk, he leaned in to get into his partner's face. "But I still don't see the connection."

Phelps put down a copy of the 1983 Dodger Annual yearbook for his favorite baseball team, pressed his thin lips together and sighed. The sigh sounded as if it came straight from his toes. "The kind of sick where she needs her family around her, doing stuff for her."

Bryce still didn't see the problem. "So? Bring her out here. You've got those extra bedrooms since your kids went off to college—" He didn't get a chance to finish.

Phelps eyed him as if he'd lost his mind. "Look, I feel bad for her, but there's no way that harpy's moving in with us. Not unless you wanna see my face on a mug shot posted in Homicide with the words 'Rogue Cop' over it."

Bryce was trying very hard to understand what the other man was saying. "So what's the plan? You and Alice're moving in with her?"

Phelps shivered. "Different scenario, same results. Alice and I are renting a place up there."

"There" being Fresno, Bryce recalled.

"She's going to play Florence What's-Her-Name and I guess I'm gonna see if I can finally write that crime thriller I'm always talking about." The contented, wistful expression on his face faded and Phelps got back to the present. "Officially, for now I'm taking an extended leave of absence. Don't look so glum. I'll be back," Phelps promised. "After all, you never forget your first," he added with a wicked grin, followed by a heartfelt sigh.

Bryce shot the man a look that said he wasn't amused. "Seriously, just how long is this 'extended' leave going to be?"

Bony shoulders rose and fell beneath the loose-fitting jacket. "A few months. Six on the outside. Doctors say that the old girl's on her way out. Could be anytime now," he said a little wistfully. And then reality set in. "'Course, she's got the constitution of a rock. She just might hang around for another ten, twenty years just to stick it to me." Phelps laughed dryly as he put the last of his things into the cardboard box.

He paused. "Not everybody's as lucky as you are,

partner. Your family gets along and they all have each other's backs no matter what." He picked up the box then put it back down again and, only half kidding, said, "Any chance I could get adopted? I wouldn't take up much space."

Bryce laughed and shook his head. "Yeah, I'll be sure to ask." And then he sobered as he scanned the squad room. "It won't seem the same without you."

"Yeah, yeah, you'll forget about me the second I walk out the door." Phelps saw that his partner was looking at something or someone over his shoulder. Turning, he saw a slender blonde crossing the threshold, a miniature version of his cardboard box in her hands. "Sooner, maybe," he commented. "Well, off I go." He put his hand into Bryce's, shaking it. "It's been good. Maybe with luck, I'll see you soon."

And then Phelps looked around. "Anyone know where I can pick up some hemlock, cheap?" he asked, raising his voice so that it carried to the rest of the inhabitants of the squad room.

A cacophony of voices answered him as he made his way, nodding through the maze of desks and detectives, toward the exit.

He passed the blonde who was walking in. Assuming that she was there to take his place, Phelps nodded in her direction and, in a low voice, said, "The desk's in the rear of the room. So's your partner." And then he smiled broadly. "Good luck with that."

Scottie's arm tightened around the small box she was carrying. It was only half filled, but she hadn't been able to find a smaller box when she'd cleaned out her space in Homicide.

The transfer had come through so quickly, Scottie thought, it had almost taken her breath away. She'd been prepared to make several requests and to write long petitions before she got the okay to make the transfer from Homicide to Robbery. She'd been certain she would have to plead her case and be movingly convincing before the approval was given. After all, she'd been fairly certain she had done a more than decent job in Homicide.

She'd certainly managed to clear all her cases. But then, on the other hand, Aurora was not exactly a snake pit of crime. It habitually made the FBI's top ten list of safest US cities for its size and she liked to think she was part of the reason for that. She worked hard, kept to herself and never challenged authority. As far as she knew, that was the winning formula for a valuable employee.

She'd thought that her commanding officer would have put up more of a fuss about losing her. But to her surprise, after she'd put in her request, stating only that she felt rather burned out working Homicide—it was the only thing that occurred to her to use as her reason for requesting the transfer—it had been granted the next morning. The captain hadn't even tried to talk her out of it.

Her partner, Joe Mathias, had appeared a little surprised as well as dismayed when he'd learned she was transferring, but not enough to try to get her to change her mind or to attempt to block the transfer.

They had worked well together, but only in the way that two cogs located on the same machine worked well. They had never socialized after hours—her choice—and they didn't even know any personal details about one another—also her choice. Mathias had tried—he had pictures of his wife and kids on his desk and on occasion would tell her about something he and his family had done over the weekend—but Scottie had zealously kept her private life just that.

Private.

Part of the reason for her secrecy was that she didn't want anyone to find out about Ethan. He was not only her half brother, at one point she had also been his legal guardian. Her gut instincts had her hiding their connection—just in case.

And now "just in case" had happened—maybe.

For now, it proved to her that she'd been right about deciding to keep her private life under wraps. If her hunch was right, and Ethan was involved in what was now going on, there'd be no way that she would be allowed to work on the break-ins that had suddenly begun to plague the good citizens living in some of the more upscale neighborhoods of Aurora.

If anyone knew about Ethan and the nefarious life he had supposedly left behind, she would be barred from doing any sort of investigation that could clear his name—*if* Ethan was part of this. It was a phrase she kept hanging on to. She still had no actual proof that he was involved.

But then there was her gut, which compelled her to move forward. Always forward for him—just in case.

* * *

Newly seated, Bryce rose again to get a better look at the woman taking long, measured steps as she crossed the squad room. Just the faintest of hip movement marked every step she took.

He had trouble drawing his eyes away.

His first thought was that she was a hell of what his grandfather would have referred to as "a looker." His second was that she was one of the city's residents coming in to file a complaint involving goods stolen during the execution of some sort of a robbery.

But then he took a second look at the box in her hands, a far smaller one than Phelps had used to carry out his possessions, but still a box. That caused Bryce to reassess his initial take.

As he watched the leggy blonde walk in his direction, Bryce was vaguely aware that he wasn't the only one assessing the woman. Small wonder. The statuesque blonde had a no-nonsense gait that captured a man's attention from the very first moment she entered his line of sight. Slender, she was wearing a straight, light gray skirt that stopped a few inches above her knee, making her look as if she was all leg.

And what legs! he caught himself thinking. They were the kind of legs that walked right into a man's dreams and had him fantasizing all sorts of things he had no business fantasizing about—*especially* if it turned out that there was some sort of a working relationship that had to happen.

Snapping out of his momentary reverie, Bryce

crossed over to the newcomer as he summoned his most inviting smile.

"Can I help you?" he asked.

The low voice he heard in response sounded as if it had been wrapped in honey and dipped in warm whiskey before being poured over a glass of ice.

"With what?"

The woman's response caught him off guard. Bryce heard himself say the first two things that came into his head. "With the box you're holding. With finding whoever you're looking for. Anything," he concluded, leaving the offer open-ended.

"The box isn't heavy," she replied, tightening her hold on the box with its meager contents—just a few basic manuals she'd found useful during the execution of her job. "And I'm not looking for a 'who,' I'm looking for a desk."

The grin was instantaneous, widening his mouth to reveal two rows of snowstorm-white teeth. "Fortunately the one next to mine just happens to be empty," Bryce told her, pivoting on the ball of his foot and doing a 180 so that he was once again facing the direction he had come from.

"Fortunately," Scottie echoed, her emotionless tone giving no indication she thought it was anything of the kind.

Since he had pointed to the newly vacated desk, Scottie walked toward it. Bryce was right behind her. He took the opportunity to drink in every nuance of her body from that vantage point before hurrying to catch up so that he could at least be at her side when she set her things down.

Which he was.

"I guess you're taking Detective Phelps's place," Bryce said as she put the small box on the desk.

Ordinarily, Bryce didn't have to search for an icebreaker or an opening line. In his experience, women, even those who were as easy on the eyes as this one was, didn't need much encouragement when it came to making conversation. They were usually all too eager to do three-quarters of the talking, if not more.

But this one was different. She didn't seem inclined to talk, which in itself was unusual. Unlike a couple of his brothers, Bryce had never fancied himself to be the strong, silent type. Besides, he'd found that the more someone talked, the more they wound up revealing about themselves. He had never been one who cared for surprises.

He liked knowing things right from the start, liked having things all laid out in front of him, nice and visible.

The blonde at Phelps's desk obviously didn't subscribe to that philosophy. At least, it didn't seem that way.

"Apparently," the leggy blonde said as she almost bonelessly slid into Phelps's chair.

Having gotten involved in observing what was nothing short of poetry in motion, Bryce blinked then narrowed his eyes slightly as he looked at the newcomer.

"Excuse me?"

Scottie recreated the last two bits of dialogue. "You said it looked like I was taking Phelps's place. I said 'apparently.' There," she announced in a tone that was nothing short of dismissive. "I think that we're all caught up."

Bryce pulled over his own chair, positioning it so that it was inches away from facing hers, and then straddled it. He crossed his arms over the top of the creased black padding as he looked at her. His sharp green eyes all but bored right into her, giving the impression that he could glimpse everything clear down to the bone, every thought, every fear, *everything*.

"All caught up?" Bryce echoed with just the slightest bit of mockery in his voice. "No, I don't think so. Not by a long shot." And then his easygoing manner returned as he asked, "Don't you want to know my name?"

Soft, expressive blue eyes rose to look into his. "Bryce Cavanaugh," she replied.

Bryce's amused grin widened. So she'd done her homework. But why? *Was* this woman his new partner? And how did everyone but him know that he was *getting* a new partner?

"Okay, so you know my name," Bryce conceded. "Don't you want to know anything else?"

The same slightly disinterested tone she'd used before now accompanied the single word that emerged next from her lips.

"No."

Undaunted, Bryce informed her, "Well, *I* want to

know some things." When his seatmate raised her eyes to his again, giving him the impression that she was waiting for his question, he asked it. "Just who the hell *are* you?"

"Detective Alexandra Scott." She stopped short of telling him that most people wound up calling her Scottie. He'd find his way to that soon enough—and if he didn't, that was okay, too. Her priority had always been solving cases, not nicknames.

"Where did you come from?" Bryce questioned, his eyes once again washing over her. Who *was* this woman and had she been around all this time without him seeing her? He *really* needed to get out more. "It's too early for Christmas, so I know it wasn't a sled with eight tiny reindeer that brought you here. Besides," he continued as if he was really being serious, "I don't think I was *that* good a boy this year to merit someone like you under my Christmas tree."

Scottie blew out a breath. If she didn't give him an answer and set him straight, this one looked as if he could go on talking nonsense like this indefinitely. There'd been a number of Cavanaughs in Homicide Division, as well, so she was well acquainted with the way they behaved.

She supposed this was what came of having a huge family to fall back on. People like that could afford to wisecrack and act as if they didn't have a care in the world.

It was different for her. All there was in her world were cares. Big cares. She'd never had anyone to fall back on. Her father had died before she was eight and her mother, it had soon became apparent, hadn't been able to keep it together for more than a few days at a time. She wound up mothering her mother as well as Ethan, who was a product of one of her mother's one-night stands.

Things had never gone smoothly, but they had gone well enough for a while. But then, in a bid for "uniqueness," Ethan had begun to act out, hanging around with this one small group until he'd gotten in trouble and gotten caught.

It was easy to see that the path he was on had only one final destination. Temporarily putting her own life on hold, she'd sued to become her brother's guardian, citing that her alcoholic, pill-popping mother was unfit. Shortly after she had, her mother had overdosed and died. That had been over seven years ago.

Scottie had refused to let herself cry. She'd just pushed on, holding down two part-time jobs, going to school online and trying to make a home for herself and Ethan. For a while, things were going all right. Ethan behaved and she wound up joining the Aurora police force.

And then Ethan had fallen back on his old ways. She'd tracked him down, dragged him back and, over the course of one very long weekend during which she'd locked herself up with Ethan, she'd managed to eventually get through to him.

He'd been out of trouble, holding down a job for close to five years.

Until now. She needed to find him before it was too late.

"I just transferred from the Homicide Division," she heard herself telling the inquisitive detective. She knew she needed to answer just enough of his questions to not arouse any undue suspicions as to her real motives for the transfer.

"By choice?" he asked.

Why was he asking her that? Did he think she had an ulterior motive for getting into his department? "Yes."

Bryce's expression was completely unreadable. "Whose?"

She looked at him quizzically for a moment before saying, "Mine."

Bryce nodded. "I can't say I blame you. It can get to you, looking at dead bodies all the time. Even one can be too many for some people."

"Thank you for your understanding," Scottie said crisply, hoping that was the end of it.

It wasn't.

Bryce made no effort to vacate his chair or move it back where it belonged. "The seat's still warm."

Scottie blinked, totally lost. "What?"

"From my last partner. He just now literally got up and walked out the door a couple minutes ago." Bryce nodded toward the doorway. "I think you even might have passed each other. Anyway," Bryce said, shifting to another topic, "I'm surprised they found a substitute so soon."

"I'm not a substitute, I'm a transfer," Scottie corrected. When she'd put in for the transfer, no one had said anything about a position being vacated.

But given the current string of break-ins, she'd just assumed that the department would be open to getting extra help.

Bryce misread her defensive tone. "I didn't mean to make that sound belittling."

Whether she liked it or not, if she was going to get along with this man, she had to get a grip. Learn the ropes. So she forced herself to flash a half-apologetic smile in his general direction.

"Sorry, it's been a rough morning," she told him vaguely.

Bryce was nothing if not a sympathetic ear. His sisters had taught him well. "Care to share?" he asked.

She'd grown up bottling up every single emotion she'd ever experienced. She'd done her best over the years to be Ethan's pillar. But no one had ever been hers. There was no way she was about to start now.

"No."

For some reason he hadn't expected her to say anything else. Bryce suppressed a laugh. Instead he said, "*Scottie*, I think this is the beginning of a beautiful friendship," paraphrasing the closing line in one of his favorite old movies, *Casablanca*.

"If you say so," Scottie replied dismissively. All she wanted to do was to settle in and get down to work.

Chapter 2

She'd never heard any talk that one of the innumerable Cavanaughs to be found within the police department was a little lacking in the cerebral area. But then, Scottie assumed that wasn't exactly a topic that anyone would bring up if they could help it. Over the years the Cavanaughs had become the very lifeblood of the police department and since the chief of detectives was a Cavanaugh—an exceptionally fair, evenhanded man, she'd heard—it seemed only prudent to not muddy the waters if it could possibly be avoided.

Still, in her opinion, the detective whose desk was butted up against hers seemed far too prone to just smile for no particular reason, like some sort of happy idiot.

She supposed he could be on the level.

What was it like, she wondered, just to be happy for no reason at all?

Was it even *possible*?

Great, only five minutes into her transfer and she was already waxing philosophical, Scottie upbraided herself. If she wasn't careful, she was in real danger of turning into one of those people she had always disliked and thought of as useless. People who lived to contemplate absolutely nothing of consequence and went on about it ad infinitum.

Quickly putting away the few things she had brought with her from her old desk, Scottie was acutely aware of the fact that Bryce Cavanaugh was still hovering over her like a drone trying to decide just where to finally strike.

Scottie shut her middle drawer and focused her attention on the handsome, annoying man looming over her.

"Is there something I can help you with?" she asked in a crisp, distant voice.

Bryce's smile was nothing if not affable. "No, I kind of thought it might be the other way around."

Her eyes narrowed. "I don't need any help," she informed him.

"I was just volunteering to take you to Lieutenant Handel and introduce you." For just a fleeting second he thought he saw a silent query in the blonde's laser blue eyes. "You know, the guy who barks out the orders and sends us out on our assignments. It's usually protocol to report to him first thing when you join his squad."

Damn, she'd forgotten all about that. She hated slipping up like this. She was usually so detail-oriented. But she'd been so consumed with trying to locate Ethan and head him off—if this really *was* Ethan's work—as well as getting transferred to Robbery that she'd forgotten all about the final steps involved in a department transfer.

Scottie took a deep breath, pulling herself together as subtly as possible.

"Right," she lied, "I was just getting to that. I didn't want to just leave my things all over the place when I went to check in with the commanding officer."

She rose and so did Bryce.

His attention entirely on his new partner, Bryce pushed his chair back toward his desk without sparing it a single glance. It still came to rest in the right place. "Let's go," he said.

"I don't need an escort." She thought she'd already made that clear. "Just point out his office." Although she actually had a fairly good idea where to find the squad leader.

Everyone was out in the open. As with the Homicide Division, the person in charge occupied a glass office located against the wall farthest from the squad room's entrance. Originality was not exactly the department's strong suit.

"I was taught it wasn't polite to point," he told her, humor glinting his green eyes.

He'd almost be cute if he wasn't so damn annoying, Scottie thought. But he *was* annoying and, besides, she wasn't in the market for cute. She was in the market to either put her mind at ease about Ethan or, barring that, to clear Ethan's name and extricate him, if possible, from any kind of mess he had allowed himself to get mixed up in. "Cute" had no place in that.

Bryce's smile widened. "Humor me. You'll find I can be a very useful guy," he added, hoping that was the end of the discussion.

Scottie had learned to work alone. A partner, especially one who apparently fancied himself as God's gift to womankind as this one so obviously did, would only get in her way in more ways than she could count. But she didn't want to commemorate her first day in the department by butting heads with one of the Cavanaughs—especially since it looked as if the man *was* going to be her partner.

Could it get any worse? Scottie asked herself.

The question no sooner occurred to her than the answer came to her. It could be a lot worse—if Ethan was actually involved in these break-ins.

She stifled a shiver, trying not to go there mentally.

"Lead the way, Useful Guy," she told Bryce, making no attempt to hide the sarcasm in her voice.

This is going to get interesting, Bryce thought, amused while he did exactly as she requested.

Since the door to the tiny room was open, Bryce paused to knock on the office door frame then stuck his head into the lieutenant's space. "You got a minute, Loo?" he asked.

"Not since I signed on to take over this department," the older man lamented.

Pausing and saving the screen he was working on, Lieutenant Mike Handel, father of three and twenty-one-year veteran with the department, turned his chair fifteen degrees to the left and looked at the two occupants standing in his cubbyhole of an office.

"Yes?"

"Phelps just left," Bryce informed his superior. Then, gesturing toward the woman beside him, he said, "And this appears to be his replacement."

Handel half rose in his chair in a minor show of respect. Gaunt, with what looked to be a two-day shadow, he appeared to be impressed. "Nice to know that Personnel can operate so efficiently. I don't recall even sending down the proper request form to Human Resources for a replacement."

"You didn't," Scottie said, speaking up. "It was just serendipity. I asked for the transfer."

The lieutenant smiled but his expression beneath the smile was unreadable.

"'Serendipity,'" he repeated. "Now there's a word you don't hear every day. I'm Lieutenant Handel," he told the young woman standing in front of his desk. He extended his hand to her.

"Detective Alexandra Scott," Scottie replied, taking the hand the man offered and shaking it.

"Tell me, 'Detective Alexandra Scott,' I'm curious…"

Handel asked, sitting again. "Did you request to be transferred *into* Robbery or *out of* Homicide?"

Scottie paused only for a second before answering. "A little of both, sir."

Handel nodded. "Good answer—except for the 'sir' part. 'Sir' is for my father and the Chief of Ds. If you want my attention, just say 'Loo.'" And then Handel put his hand out again, waiting.

Belatedly, Scottie remembered that she was still holding on to her transfer orders along with a file containing a thumbnail summary of her police service background.

"Sorry," she murmured, placing the file in front of him on the desk.

"Nothing to be sorry about, Detective." Opening the file, Handel skimmed through it quickly then looked up at her again. "Everything seems to be in order, Detective. I take it that you already know you'll be partnering up with Cavanaugh here."

Scottie didn't pretend to smile at the prospect. "Yes, sir—um, Loo. But I thought I should mention that I work better alone."

Mentally, Scottie crossed her fingers even though she had a feeling that it was hopeless.

Just as she'd guessed, her statement had less than no effect on her new commanding officer.

"Superman works alone. The rest of us work in pairs. Except for me. I work with *all* of you. Trust me," Handel went on, "in this department, you'll need all the help that you can get. Stupid criminals exist mostly in amusing anecdotes in *Reader's Digest*.

Today's breed of thief is smarter, quicker and way sharper than the thief from your father's generation."

Scottie was still standing at military attention. "I'll keep that in mind, si—Loo."

Handel laughed, clearly tickled by her struggle to address him correctly.

"Work on that, Detective. You'll get the hang of it." And then Handel turned to look at Bryce. "Why don't you help the new kid here catch up on what you and some of the others have been working on?" he suggested.

"You got it, Loo," Bryce answered, more than ready to accommodate his superior. He and Scottie turned, beginning to leave the small inner office.

"Oh, Scott," Handel suddenly called out.

Scottie turned and glanced at the man, wondering if he was having second thoughts about her transfer or if there was something else that was wrong. She had learned, long ago, never to expect smooth sailing even if the surface of the lake was as smooth as glass.

"Yes, Loo?"

Because she hadn't stuttered and stumbled over his name, Handel smiled his approval then told her what he'd wanted to say. "Welcome aboard."

"Thank you," she murmured.

She followed her new partner out.

"He takes a little getting used to," Bryce confided as if he could read her thoughts. *As do you, probably*, Bryce added silently.

"No more than anyone else," she replied with

a vague shrug. "Everybody's got their rules and quirks."

"What are yours?" he asked as they got back to their desks.

"I've just got two," she told him simply. "Rules, not quirks," she clarified. "Do a good job and never mix work with home. Can we get to work now?" she asked, signaling an end to any exchange he thought they might be making.

"Absolutely. I take it that you're aware of the series of break-ins that have been going on these last few weeks," Bryce said, pulling his chair up a little closer to her desk as he lowered his voice just a shade.

She'd been the one to request they get to work, yet the question he'd just led with seemed almost out of the blue. So much so that it almost appeared he was asking her personally rather than just as a general introduction to the case she would be working.

Ever mindful of the possibility that Ethan was involved in these break-ins, her main concern was that, somehow, the connection would be made and once it was known that she was Ethan's sister—even his half sister—she wouldn't be allowed to work to clear his name.

"Why?" she responded uneasily, watching Bryce's every move.

Bryce studied his new partner. Suddenly she appeared rather jumpy. Was that because she was the new kid on the block or was there something else going on that he needed to look into? Something he needed to know about before things went any further, both in the investigation and besides that?

After a moment he chalked up her momentary display of nerves to her wanting to do well on her first assignment in the new division. He couldn't exactly blame her for that.

"Because it's all over the news these days, for one thing," he explained, still covertly studying her reaction to this whole scenario.

"Oh, right. Sorry," she apologized. And then she knew just how to play this—survival in all sorts of situations had taught her that. "I had too much coffee this morning and I guess I just want to carry my weight right off the bat. Didn't mean to sound jumpy."

"Don't worry, you'll have plenty of opportunity to carry your own weight—and mine, too," he added with a chuckle. "I've got a list of people who've come home to find that they've been paid a little visit by our local friendly break-in artists. It's here somewhere." As he spoke, he began searching through the various files on his desk.

The files looked as if they'd been dropped on his desk by a passing hurricane. Nothing seemed to be organized.

In her opinion Cavanaugh had an awful lot of unnecessary papers scattered over on his desk. It became abundantly clear that the papers were stuck into files in no particular order, either. Finding just one specific thing would be like going on a wild-goose chase.

Finally she couldn't hold her tongue any longer. "Wouldn't you have more luck if you had all that on the computer?" she asked.

He countered her suggestion with a list of reasons why he hadn't had anyone input the material into files on the computer. He was computer literate, but he had never become a fanatic about it.

"Paper files don't suffer glitches or suddenly become unavailable because of power outages. Besides," he said, sparing her a grin before going back to the hunt, "this way's easier."

Her eyes swept over the haphazard piles of files. "If you say so," she murmured.

Eventually, Bryce laid his hands on everything he was looking for. He in turn handed them all over to his new partner.

For her part, Scottie spent the rest of the morning and most of the afternoon going through the various files that Bryce, his former partner and a couple of other detectives in the squad room had compiled.

There had been eight break-ins in this latest wave of home robberies. All the robberies had taken place in Aurora's more exclusive, upper-end neighborhoods. That was the one thing all the incidents had in common. The only other thing they had in common—for now—was that there had been no one home at the time of the break-ins.

But beyond that, nothing seemed similar to her. The people who'd had their space violated had no common thread running through all their lives. They didn't attend the same church, didn't shop in the same stores and they didn't send their children to the same schools. Two of the victims were single men, while the other five were families.

At first glance the break-ins seemed to all be just random invasions, haphazardly picked, but Scottie knew better than that. There had to be a common thread running through them, something that had drawn the thief's attention in the first place, like a theme, or a memory, or payback for something.

She just prayed that the common thread running through all these home invasions wasn't Ethan.

For the umpteenth time Scottie slipped her phone out of her pocket and swiped the screen, bringing it to life. She checked her texts and then her voice messages.

Nothing.

Ethan hadn't called her back, hadn't texted. Something was wrong, she *knew* it.

The old Ethan, the one she'd had to bail out of jail on more than one occasion before he'd finally come to his senses, wouldn't have called her back. He would have carelessly ignored her messages until it suited his schedule to call her back. But the *new* Ethan, the one who was finally amounting to something, the one who gave meaning to her life, he would have definitely called her back. He would have called her the moment she'd left her first message.

It occurred to her that she hadn't heard from Ethan in a month.

She'd just chalked it up to his being busy. She didn't

want him to feel as if she was breathing down his neck, but she really did want to know where he was.

Where are you, Ethan? she silently demanded as she stared at her phone.

"Checking for messages from your boyfriend?" Bryce asked.

Scottie swung her chair around, narrowly avoiding hitting the detective smack in his knees.

"Don't you make any noise when you sneak up on people?" she accused.

"I think the answer to that is self-explanatory, otherwise it wouldn't be called 'sneaking.' But since I have your attention, I was just curious. You've checked your phone at least once every hour since you started working those files. Hot date?" he asked, amused.

"To answer your question, no, I'm not checking for messages from my boyfriend. I don't have a boyfriend, consequently there is no 'hot date,'" Scottie informed him rather coldly.

Now *that*, Bryce thought, he found very hard to believe, given the way the woman looked.

But he let the topic drop, to be followed up some other time.

"Well, it's time to call it a day, anyway. Why don't you join me for a drink at Malone's?" he suggested.

Malone's, run by a retired policeman, was where more than one officer of the law could be found unwinding and temporarily setting down the burdens of the day. Bryce assumed she was familiar with it since, at one time or another, they'd all frequented the establishment.

"I thought we could celebrate your first day on the job. I'm buying," he added, hoping that would erase any objections she might voice at the idea.

Scottie shook her head. "Thanks, but I'll have to pass. I have somewhere else I have to be."

Before he could ask her where, Scottie had picked up her slim messenger bag, slung the strap over her shoulder and walked quickly out of the squad room.

Chapter 3

It wasn't until a couple of minutes later, when he started to leave the squad room himself, that Bryce saw the cell phone still laying on his new partner's desk. The cell's black case made it easily blend in with the desktop.

Snatching it up, Bryce quickly hurried out of the squad room and to the elevator to catch up with his new partner. But he was too late. She had already gotten on and went down.

Not bothering to wait for another elevator car to arrive—that would only cost him more time—Bryce opted for the stairs. He fairly flew down the three flights to the ground floor. But as he emerged out of the stairwell, he found the elevator car standing open and empty. Scottie was nowhere to be seen. She must have just left the building.

Just how fast did this woman move?

Not bothering to contemplate the question, Bryce exited the building via the rear entrance. The second he got out, he saw Scottie in the distance. She was just getting into her car. He whistled and called out her name, but she obviously didn't hear him.

Bryce regarded the phone in his hand. He supposed he could just give her the cell phone tomorrow when she came in. That would be the simplest thing to do. But since cell phones were no longer just phones but the owner's vital connection to the world, Bryce decided to give it one more try and go after her.

Pocketing the cell, Bryce hurried over to his own vehicle and got into it. After he started the car, he went out the same way he assumed his partner had.

When he left the lot, he just barely managed to catch sight of her silver subcompact making a right at the corner.

Employing his best tailing skills, Bryce followed the silver Honda for several blocks. He made sure to keep one car length behind her. He knew that he could just speed up, flip on his siren and catch up to her, but he had to admit his curiosity had been aroused. Just where else was it that his partner just "had to be" that had caused her to turn down a friendly drink and forget to take her phone?

Keeping her in his sights, Bryce wound up following his new partner beyond the city limits into the next city. Vaguely familiar with the area, he saw that she was driving toward a less than upscale neighborhood.

Just where the hell is she going at this time of day in this area?

By the time he saw Scottie's car pull into a parking lot, his curiosity was not just aroused but fully engaged. Especially when he looked around and realized she had parked right in front of a homeless shelter.

That did *not* look like the kind of place someone like Scottie would go to, he thought. At least not unless she was following a lead.

Could that be it? Had she picked up something in all those files he'd given her to review and not said anything to him? Just exactly how much of a Lone Ranger was this woman?

Needing answers, Bryce pulled his car up into the lot and parked several spaces away from hers in the first spot he could find. Shutting off his engine, he sat back and waited.

And waited.

Since it was still light out, it allowed him to absorb the details of the squat, two-story building and its surrounding area. He supposed, as far as homeless shelters went, this one looked to be in decent repair. As he sat, he watched several people enter the building, all looking as if what they needed most was a bath and a container of hope.

Thirty-five minutes later, he saw the door open from the inside and watched as Scottie finally came out. He snapped to attention. She did *not* look happy, he noted.

Judging from the scowl on her face, she appeared to be frustrated.

"Okay, time for some answers," Bryce muttered to himself as he got out of his car.

Ever alert, the sudden movement caught her eye and Scottie swung around to face it. When she realized who it was, she frowned. Deeply.

What the hell was *he* doing here?

Incensed, she strode quickly toward the man and his vehicle.

"Are you following me?" Scottie challenged, not bothering to hide the fact that she was less than happy about the prospect of finding him there, obviously watching her.

"As a matter of fact, yes, I am," Bryce admitted, seeing no reason to hide the fact. "It didn't start out that way but, well, here we are."

Didn't he even have the decency to be embarrassed about being caught?

"Where the hell do you get off, following me?" Scottie demanded. By this point, she was standing next to Cavanaugh, glaring up into his face, her eyes shooting daggers. "Is this some kind of weird hobby of yours? I can't think of a single reason for you to be following me."

He appeared completely unfazed by her growing anger even though it looked as if she was going to explode at any moment.

"Can't you? Try harder," he coaxed. In response, he saw her anger spike up to another level.

"What is this, a game to you? Are you hazing me? Hazing the newcomer, is that it?" She struggled not to shout the question into his face. "Because I'm not a newcomer. I've been on the force for five years and I have—"

Part of him wondered just how angry she could get and just what she would wind up ultimately threatening him with. But if he let her detonate like that, there'd be no coming back. And it wasn't exactly going to guarantee that they'd work well together. No, he needed to dial this back a bit because they *were* obviously going to be working together, at least until she transferred again.

She appeared to be on the verge of sputtering.

Reaching into his pocket, Bryce took out her phone and held it aloft before her.

"Have you tried to make a call since you left the precinct?" he asked, effectively cutting off her budding tirade.

Her growing anger came to a screeching halt. Silence suddenly slammed into the moment. She stared, dumbfounded, at the object in his hand.

In a far more subdued voice, Scottie said, "That's my cell phone." Confused, she raised her eyes to his again.

"That's what it is, all right," he agreed amicably, his expression giving no indication that he had just been on the receiving end of hot words.

She looked confused. "What are you doing with it?"

"Trying to return it to you," he told her mildly. "You left it on your desk when you walked out and I thought you might need it," he explained. "I tried to catch up with you but you really move fast for a woman in high heels." There was a note of amused admiration in his voice.

Scottie said the first thing that came to her mind. "Why didn't you just call out my name?"

Completely embarrassed, she could almost *feel* the color rising to her cheeks. She'd practically jumped down his throat and ripped out his tongue, and apparently all he was trying to do was a good deed.

She had to get a grip, Scottie chided herself. Going off the deep end wasn't going to do Ethan any good and it could terminate her career, commendations or no commendations.

"I did, but I couldn't get your attention. And I couldn't very well call or text you, either," he added with a grin. He handed over the phone to Scottie. "These days, people have their entire lives on their phone and I figured you might want yours back."

"Thanks," she murmured. Taking the cell, she tucked it into her messenger bag. "I owe you one," she tacked on ruefully.

Bryce shrugged. "Have that drink with me at Malone's and we'll call it even."

Malone's again. She was tempted to ask this bright and upstanding representative of the Cavanaughs why it was so important to him that they have a drink together, but since he had obviously gone out of his way to get her phone to her, instead of questioning him about what was undoubtedly looked upon as a tradition by Cavanaugh and his crew, she decided to just go along with things.

"Okay," she finally replied. "If that's what it takes, I'll have that beer with you."

Her wording caught his attention. "So then we'll be even, is that what you mean?"

"I don't see it that way," she admitted, "but since you went out of your way like this to reunite me with my phone and, for some reason I don't understand, having a drink after work means something to you, and since I am in your debt, the answer to your invitation is yes." Having agreed, she pressed her lips together. "I'll follow you there."

She expected Bryce to get into his car, but he remained where he was. "Table or stool?" he wanted to know.

Scottie stared at him. Was this some kind of code? "Excuse me?"

"If you're following me," he patiently explained, "that means I'll get there first. I just wanted to know if you would rather sit at a table or take a stool at the bar?"

A table represented more privacy, a small haven from the general press of bodies and the noise, but a bar stool, while implying brevity to her also left her out in the open and vulnerable. She liked neither choice so she shrugged. "Surprise me."

He studied her for a moment. Part of him felt she had no intention of showing up, which had him wondering a host of other things he hadn't quite nailed down yet, but he wasn't about to stand out there in the parking lot, negotiating details.

"I'll do my best," he told her with a wide, inviting smile.

The man obviously thought he was too good-looking for his own good, Scottie decided as she made her way to her car. Reaching it, she turned in his direction and waved her hand, indicting that he could go.

He didn't. Instead he waited until her vehicle drew closer to his and then he put his car into drive and pulled out of the parking space.

Glancing in his rearview mirror, he saw that Scottie was indeed following him.

How long was that going to last? he mused, still not certain he could take her at her word—which in turn would bode rather badly for their fledgling work relationship. A man had to trust his partner, otherwise his life wouldn't be worth the proverbial plug nickel for long.

Bryce drove slowly, as if he was a sixteen-year-old driver with a brand-new learner's permit going on a maiden run under his father's watchful eye. Approaching intersections, if the light had turned yellow, he came to a full stop instead of pressing down harder on the accelerator to make it through before the light went red. Looking back over his life, Bryce couldn't remember *ever* driving as slowly as he did tonight.

Consequently, it felt like getting to Malone's took

forever, but finally he found himself pulling into the parking lot.

He parked in the first space he found, then got out quickly and looked over his shoulder to see if his partner was still behind him.

A silver Honda was just pulling into the lot.

"Son of a gun. Yes, Virginia, there *is* a Santa Claus," he murmured to himself, grinning. She'd actually followed him, he thought, astonished.

Parking her car, Scottie got out and then wove in and out of the rows of vehicles, making her way toward Malone's front entrance and, apparently, to Cavanaugh who was just standing there, watching her every move.

A lesser woman would have felt self-conscious, but it had never been about looks for Scottie. Everything else had always been too important for her to waste any time worrying about her appearance or spending hours fussing with her hair. She had a living to earn and a brother to raise.

She'd done progressively better and better with the first part. The second part, not so much, she thought now. She'd showed Ethan's photo to everyone at the shelter, but no one had seen her brother. The shelter had once been his go-to place when he'd wanted her to find him. Helping out at the shelter in turn seemed to help him and center him.

He was a good guy, she thought. He just needed help to stay the course.

"I thought you were going to find someplace for us to sit," she said to Bryce as she approached.

"Changed my mind," he said mildly. "I thought I'd wait since you might have trouble finding me once you were inside."

"I wouldn't have any trouble, I'd just follow the light from your aura," she quipped.

Rather than get his back up, or take offense, Bryce seemed amused by her wisecrack. "And here I thought I'd hidden it so well."

She wasn't about to stand out there, talking half the night away. She reached for the door. "Okay, let's get this over with."

"'Over with'?" he repeated. "This isn't a root canal, Scottie. It's just two partners having a drink together, getting to know each other." Turning from her, he reached for the heavy oak door, opened it and then stood there holding it for her.

She glanced at him over her shoulder just before she crossed the threshold.

"I don't need to 'get to know' you. I know all I need to know about you," she informed him.

"Probably not," he countered easily. "And I know that I know next to *nothing* about you," he said as he ushered her into the large room.

For a moment Scottie stood just inside the bar. She'd been on the force for five years, but this was her first time inside the bar most of the other officers and detectives frequented.

Depending on the day of the week, Malone's was full to varying degrees of that word. Tonight, a Wednesday, it was all but teeming with patrons, men and women who made it their life's business to keep the residents of the city safe and secure in their beds.

Slowly looking around, Scottie saw a number of people she recognized, people she had formerly worked side by side with in Homicide. She saw the surprised looks on several of their faces.

They obviously hadn't expected to see her there. Well, no more surprised than she was to find herself there, Scottie thought. She promised herself that she would have one bottle of beer with Bryce Cavanaugh—probably not the entire contents—and then, her so-called debt repaid, she'd be free to go.

When she felt the hand on her elbow, her first reaction was to pull away. She actually tried, but the hand just took a tighter hold.

"Easy, Scottie, I'm not trying to take your elbow from you, I'm just guiding you over to that table," Bryce whispered against her ear.

He did so because the noise level inside Malone's was steadily increasing and he instinctively knew she wouldn't want attention drawn to her by having him raise his voice so she could hear him. He had no way of knowing that getting so close to her, whispering so that his breath glided along her neck, would cause Scottie to unexpectedly feel something that had her instantly bracing herself.

But, braced or not, it was too late, Scottie realized. She could feel something stirring as if in automatic response.

Not the time, not the time, Scottie harshly told

herself, tamping down the feeling that had no place in her life right now.

Her entire focus had to be on Ethan, on finding him and, if it came to it, saving him, although she was still fervently praying there was some acceptable reason why he wasn't home, why he wasn't picking up his cell phone.

A reason that had nothing to do with these break-ins.

"This okay?" Bryce was asking her.

It took her a second to focus and realize what Bryce was saying. They were at a small table for two. It looked to be almost intimate if it wasn't for the fact that there was so much noise surrounding them. She supposed this was as good as anyplace.

"Sure, why not?" she said with a shrug.

"Good answer," he remarked with a smile. "What's your poison?"

Scottie never hesitated. "Pushy partners who won't back off."

The corners of his mouth curved in amusement. She was feisty, he thought. He was raised with feisty women. Anything less would have been exceedingly dull. "I meant to drink."

She gave him the name of a currently popular beer.

"That's a new one on me. Is that any good?" Bryce asked.

"Better than most. I'm not much of a drinker," she told him.

Even though there was so much noise building around them, his laugh wasn't lost in the din. Instead it seemed to undulate right through her, like a shiver waiting to happen.

"I already picked up on that," Bryce told her. His grin intensified. "See, I'm learning things about you already." The table was several feet away from the bar itself. "Stay right here," he requested. "I'll be right back."

With that, he made his way to the bar to order their drinks.

Scottie glanced over her shoulder at the front door.

Chapter 4

This would be a perfect time to make a getaway, Scottie thought. Cavanaugh's back was to her and he was busy trying to get the bartender's attention. The latter was taking and filling orders like a house afire, but it still looked as if it might take him at least a few minutes to get to Cavanaugh.

If she slipped away now…

If she slipped away now, Cavanaugh would undoubtedly hunt her down and insist on collecting his "debt" at some other, probably less convenient, time. Scottie sighed. She might as well resign herself to getting this over with and out of the way.

It wasn't easy, but she stayed where she was.

Cavanaugh came back faster than she thought he would, a mug of beer in each hand.

"You're still here," Bryce said. There actually was a note of surprise in his voice.

That made two of them, Scottie thought.

"I said that I would have that drink with you," she reminded Cavanaugh. "What, did you think I'd make a break for it?"

She found herself, just for a moment and very reluctantly, being drawn in to the man's genial smile. It was just this side of sexy and difficult to ignore.

"It crossed my mind, yes," he answered.

Her eyes met his. Maybe ground rules were called for here. "When I say I'll do something, I do it."

Bryce placed her mug of beer in front of her and then, straddling his chair, set his mug down where he was sitting.

"Good to know." He raised his mug, waiting for her to do the same. When she didn't, he went ahead with his toast. "Well, here's to a fruitful partnership."

Scottie knew she couldn't very well ignore the sentiment behind that, so she nodded, raised her mug and clinked it against his.

Taking a sip, she placed her drink down again. Glancing at her watch, she wondered how long she would have to remain at Malone's before Cavanaugh would call them square and let her leave.

"So, do you do that often?" Bryce asked out of the blue.

Caught off guard, she stared at him, quickly reviewing their sparse conversation. She came up empty. "Do what?"

"Serve dinner at the homeless shelter. I assume

that was what you were doing there." He hadn't seen her carry in any bags of clothes to donate, so he had come to the only conclusion he could about her thirty-five-minute visit to the shelter. "Very noble, by the way," he added.

She frowned. What she'd heard about the Cavanaughs was true. Once they latched on to something, they just wouldn't let go. She was going to have to answer him.

"Before you start fitting me for a halo," she told Bryce, "I wasn't there serving dinner."

"Oh?" He watched her over the rim of his mug. "Then what were you doing at the homeless shelter?"

The words "none of your business" rose to her lips, but antagonizing Cavanaugh from the get-go would just cause problems and she already had more than enough of those. So, she grudgingly told her partner, "I was looking for someone."

The look in his eyes told her that his interest had piqued a notch higher. "Who?"

Okay, this had gone as far as she was willing to go with it. "Correct me if I'm wrong, but what I do off duty is my own business."

If she'd offended him, she saw no indication. "No, you've got that right. I was just going to volunteer to help you find that 'someone,' that's all."

He couldn't help her, not without her opening up about Ethan, her brother's past and her concerns that it had caught up with him again.

"I don't need help," she told him.

The last thing she needed was to have Cavanaugh

looking for her brother's whereabouts. It wouldn't take much for him to unearth a slew of things she didn't want anyone knowing. Once Cavanaugh started digging, it would be all too easy for him to make the leap from her brother and his particular set of skills to the current break-ins plaguing the city's residents.

"I don't know about that," Bryce countered. She looked up at him sharply and he explained, "Maybe it's because I was raised with so many relatives, always willing to pitch in, but to my way of thinking, *everyone* needs help at some time or other."

"Fine," she said with finality, hoping this would be the end of it. "When I decide that I need help, I'll let you know."

Bryce studied her for a moment and she could almost *feel* his eyes probing her, poking around in places he had no business being.

"Will you?" he asked. The expression on his face told her he wasn't that convinced.

She instantly responded the way she knew he wanted her to. "Absolutely."

"I thought you always told the truth." The skeptical note in his voice told her she hadn't managed to fool him.

Okay, time to go, Scottie decided. She'd done her due diligence, now she had to go home. She wasn't sure just what her next move was since no one at the shelter had heard from Ethan in several months. Hearing that had just concerned her even more. Where was he? What had caused this break in his routine?

She refused to allow panic to take center stage. If it did, then she'd be lost, not to mention that Ethan might very well be lost, as well. She had a feeling he might need her at her sharpest.

Scottie pushed back her chair. "Well, this has been fun, but I've got to get going," she told Bryce, preparing to get up.

But what she'd hoped would be a clean getaway hit a rather large stumbling block when a tall, muscular man moved right in front of her.

"Damn, it *is* you," he said, surprised and pleased at the same time. He looked to Bryce, who was still seated. "Is the end of the world coming?"

Scottie looked up and found herself staring into the face of Duncan Cavanaugh, Bryce's older brother and one of the people she had worked with on occasion while she'd been assigned to Homicide.

An incredulous expression on his face, Duncan looked at his brother. "How did you manage to talk her into coming to Malone's? She always said no when she was working Homicide."

Bryce grinned. "I guess she just finds me better company than you."

"Yeah, like that's the reason." Duncan laughed, dismissing the answer and shaking his head. He turned back to Scottie who continued to look as if she was out of her natural habitat. "Well, it's nice to see you, Scottie. Hope things are working out for you in Robbery."

"Too soon to tell," she replied quietly, unconsciously slanting a glance toward Bryce.

"Nothing's changed, I see. Honest to a fault," Duncan commented. He smiled at her. "It has its charm." It was unclear if he was referring to her honesty or to her new department. With that, he raised his bottle in a silent salute. "Carry on, little brother."

"Shouldn't you be home?" Bryce asked. When Duncan looked at him quizzically, Bryce elaborated. "Isn't Noelle due any day now?"

"Another week or so," Duncan answered. A bemused smile played on his lips. "But you know that old adage about a watched pot not boiling—"

Hearing that, Scottie couldn't help commenting, "I'm sure your wife must love being compared to a pot."

"Actually," Duncan told her, "she was the one who came up with that line when she insisted I go about my business normally. As if I could." Duncan laughed with a shake of his head. "Lucy's with her when I can't be home," he told his brother in case the latter thought he was just abandoning his wife.

"'Lucy'?" Scottie repeated.

"Noelle's grandmother," Duncan told her. "She doesn't like being called 'grandma.' Likes 'great-grandma' even less," he added with a laugh.

"Still, don't you want to be sober for your first-born?" Bryce asked.

"I *am* sober, bro. So sober that it's almost painful. This is a light ale," he told them, holding his bottle aloft. "And I've only had one, which is my limit these

days. I'm here more for the company than the liba-
tion," Duncan confided. "Like I said, Noelle doesn't
like having me hovering around her, being nervous."

"You, nervous?" Bryce echoed incredulously.
Growing up, Duncan had always been the one who
leaped first then looked, practically giving their late
mother a heart attack more than once. "I thought you
were the brother with nerves of steel."

"His nerves might be made of steel, but he's got
a heart made out of pure mush," Moira Cavanaugh,
their sister, chimed in as she joined their small circle. "Hi, I'm Moira. I have the sad fortune of being
their sister," she told Scottie, indicating both men
at the table.

Duncan was about to defend his good name when
suddenly the first few bars of a song that almost everyone was familiar with rang out. It was a march-
ing song written by John Philip Sousa. Both Bryce
and Moira looked right at Duncan who, for the first
time in his life, turned rather pale.

"It's Lucy," he cried before he even took out his
cell. "I had Valri program that ringtone for Noelle's
grandmother so I'd know it was her calling."

"Maybe she's just checking in to see when you're
coming home," Moira suggested, even though it appeared to Scottie that she was beginning to get excited, as well.

"What are the odds?" Duncan asked. Yanking
the phone out of his pocket, he almost dropped it
right in front of Scottie before he managed to get a
better grip on it and then swipe it open. "Hello? Is it

time?" he asked, his voice almost breathless. "Oh. Okay." His shoulders sagged with relief as he told the caller, "I'll pick it up on my way home. Be there in twenty minutes."

Terminating the call, Duncan saw that all eyes around the small table and beyond were on him.

"Noelle wants me to pick up some mint-chip ice cream on my way home."

Like the others, Bryce had thought it was "time." The false alarm had him laughing. "Better get going then, bro. And give my love to Noelle."

"Isn't that how this whole thing got started?" Moira quipped innocently.

Duncan waved a silencing hand at her. He left his half-consumed bottle of ale on the table, nodding at Scottie as he said, "Nice to see you finally out after hours." And with that, he made his way to the front entrance.

"I sure hope she gives birth soon," Moira commented to Bryce and his new partner as she started walking away, as well. "Right now, Duncan's moving around like a man in a trance."

"As opposed to the way he'll be moving around after the baby's here and he hasn't had a decent night's sleep in a week."

Scottie turned in her chair to see that the comment had come from Sean Cavanaugh, the head of the Crime Scene Investigation's day shift and part of the older generation of Cavanaughs working in the precinct.

Obviously having overheard their conversation,

Sean smiled warmly at the young woman at the table with his nephew.

"Poor guy doesn't know that these are what he'll look back on as 'the good old days' for the first couple of years as he struggles to get his 'daddy legs,'" Sean said with a fond laugh.

"'Daddy legs'?" Scottie repeated, looking toward the older man for an explanation.

"They're just like sea legs except they're a lot trickier to maneuver with," Sean recalled, laughing softly as he remembered several instances. "After having seven kids, I ought to know."

"I thought it was the mother who stayed up all night with the kids," Bryce commented.

His uncle laughed, patting him on his cheek. "So young, so much to learn," he commented with amusement. And then he looked at Scottie again, as if taking a close look at her this time. "You're Bryce's new partner, aren't you?"

She and Sean Cavanaugh had never crossed paths. That he even knew who she was really surprised her. "Yes, but how did you—?"

The corners of Sean's mouth curved, his expression almost bordering on the mysterious.

"There are no secrets in the police department, Detective Scott. And even less in the Cavanaugh world." His green eyes took measure of her quickly and he clearly liked what he saw. "First time here at Malone's?" he asked.

Was there a sign taped on her back that said tourist or something along those lines? Or was it that she just looked so out of place? She had to ask the man, "Now, how would you know that?"

"I head the CSI unit, Scottie. It's my job to know everything," he told her mildly. Turning toward the bartender, he signaled for the man's attention. When he got it, Sean indicated the two people sitting at the table behind him. "The next round's on me," he told the bartender.

Scottie protested immediately. "No, I just stopped in for the one."

"You don't have to drink it," Sean told her good-naturedly. "Just hold on to the bottle. 'Getting a drink at Malone's' is, for the most part, just an excuse to linger on the premises and mingle with your brothers and sisters in blue." His smile, a genial, comforting expression, widened as he added, "In my family's case, that's truer than you'd expect. Be seeing you around," he said to both Bryce and Scottie just before he walked away and left the establishment.

"Two of the same, right?" the bartender asked, depositing two more bottles at the table that she was sharing with her partner.

"I really never drink this much," Scottie told the man sitting opposite her.

"Like Uncle Sean said," Bryce reminded her, "you don't have to drink. It's just an excuse to linger."

She wanted him to get something straight right off the bat. "If I wanted to linger, I wouldn't need an excuse," Scottie told him.

His mouth quirked just a little. "The key word here being *wanted*," Bryce guessed. It was obvious that she wanted to leave. He sat back. He would have wanted her to stay a bit longer, but he wasn't about to tie her to her chair. "Well, you lived up to your bargain, so you're free to go." But before she left, in the spirit of honesty, he couldn't help telling her, "I was just hoping that once you came, you'd want to stay a bit."

Scottie had been feeling restless and antsy ever since she'd come out of the homeless shelter empty-handed. "I don't like wasting time."

Bryce gestured around to not just include their table but the surrounding people, as well. "This isn't wasting time."

She pinned him with a look. Everyone was sitting around, exchanging bits and pieces of what had once been conversation. They lived in a world of abbreviations and sound bites.

"All right, then tell me. What is it?" she asked.

"It's recharging your batteries, maybe talking things out with other law-enforcement agents who might have a clearer perspective than you do. It's clearing your head so that you can go home without keeping everything bottled up inside and scaring the person who means the most to you. At its simplest level," Bryce added, "it's networking."

She focused on the first couple of points he'd mentioned. "So that's what's going on here?" she asked, doing her best to keep the sarcasm she keenly felt from infiltrating her voice. "Crime solving?"

"At times," Bryce responded without blinking an eye. "And, like I said, at other times, it's just kicking back, unwinding and recharging. That's a lot more important than you think."

"I do that at home," she informed him and then, because it was getting noisier, she raised her voice and said, "I don't need a network to get me there."

"More power to you. Some of us, through no fault of our own, do need a little help with that, and being around other people who know what it's like to lay your life on the line 24/7 makes it just a little easier to communicate." She was leaving, he could see it in her eyes. Because his curiosity had always been unbridled, he grabbed the last chance he had and asked her one more time. "Who were you looking for at the shelter?"

His curiosity made *her* curious. "Why is it so important for you to know?" she challenged.

He repeated his offer, making it seem more appealing this time. "Because, you might have noticed, I have this huge network I can tap into."

Bryce waved his hand around the bar. There were a lot of his relatives there, as well as a lot of fellow law-enforcement agents he'd had occasion to work with. Most were great believers in the "one hand washes the other" axiom as long as no laws were broken and no one was hurt in the process.

"And if you tell me who you're looking for, I can help you find him—or her." Bryce tagged the latter on just in case she was looking for a woman.

She supposed that he meant well, even though he was prying.

"Thanks, I'll keep that in mind." Scottie rose. "Thanks for the drink."

"You didn't finish it," he pointed out, standing.

Scottie paused to drain the last of the light beer from the first serving. The round that Sean had paid for stood untouched.

Despite the speed with which she drank the last of her initial beer, she felt nothing, not even a slight buzz.

"There you go," she announced, dramatically putting the empty bottle down, then smiling up into her partner's face. "Finished."

But as she started to go, Bryce caught her by her wrist and held her in place. There was silent accusation in her blue eyes as she glared at him and tried to yank free.

"Why don't you wait a couple of minutes until that hits bottom?" Bryce suggested. One drink was nothing, but he had no idea about her tolerance for alcohol and the last thing he wanted was to have her on the road when she suddenly became light-headed and unable to navigate that little thing she called a car.

"It's light beer," Scottie protested, trying to pull away again. But he only tightened his hold on her wrist. "There's nothing to 'hit,'" she insisted.

Bryce's stance was unwavering. "Humor me," he requested.

Chapter 5

Scottie's eyes narrowed. She wasn't about to cause a scene, but she wasn't about to be bullied, either. "For how long?" Scottie quietly demanded. "Just how long do you expect me to 'humor' you?"

There was a fire about this woman that he found oddly appealing.

He had no idea why a little voice suddenly materialized in his head and whispered, *Until the end of time*. He could just hear her response to that if he told her, Bryce thought. Even without his saying anything, she appeared to be barely constrained, like a volcano that was about to blow.

"Just a few minutes," he told her.

Whether she liked it or not, he was really only thinking of her safety. If she was a novice at drink-

ing, the way she had thrown back the last third of her
beer would hit her hard any moment now.

"Define 'few,'" Scottie told him, glancing at her
watch.

Draining his own bottle, he pulled a number out
of the air. "Give me ten minutes."

She was getting impatient. She should have never
gone along with this in the first place. "I've already
given you more than that and I do have a life outside
of the police department."

Because he'd never seen her at Malone's, he'd
gotten the impression that Scottie wasn't much of a
drinker. If she wasn't, then her consuming that much
beer as quickly as she had would throw her completely off. It would definitely impair her reflexes.
He didn't want her out on the road, driving under
those circumstances.

But as he regarded her, carefully watching her expression, he saw no change taking hold, no appearance of giddiness slipping in. Maybe he was being
concerned about nothing.

"How do you feel?" he asked her.

There was no hesitation on Scottie's part as she
answered, "Irritated."

Bryce released her wrist. "I guess you're okay to
drive," he told her.

She supposed he was just trying to look out for
her. But she was so accustomed to looking out for
herself that to have someone else even hint at doing
it had her at a loss as to how to react.

Still, she felt obligated to explain her reaction, at

least to some degree. "Look, I want you to understand something. If I'd felt the slightest bit impaired, there is no way I'd put myself behind the wheel and drive. I've got too much respect for my life, the life of any unsuspecting pedestrian or driver out there and the laws of this state against driving inebriated." She paused. "Have I made myself clear?"

The woman was as headstrong as they came, Bryce thought. This was going to be one interesting partnership, to say the least.

"Perfectly."

Scottie inclined her head. "Okay, then. Thanks for the drink. I'll see you bright and early tomorrow. Unless, of course, you decide to stay here and drink everyone else under the table," she couldn't help adding, just the barest hint of a smile playing on her lips.

"That was never my intent," he assured her. And then he surprised her by asking, "Want me to walk you to your car?"

She looked at her new partner, trying to understand where he was coming from. Did she look as if she wasn't capable of finding her vehicle? Or was he somehow trying to ingratiate himself to her by behaving gallantly? Or did he think, for some reason, that this was something akin to a date?

Scottie hadn't a clue. All she knew was that she wanted to get going so she could swing by Ethan's apartment, just in case he'd finally turned up.

"No, I don't want you to walk me to my car," she told Bryce. "I want you to stay here and mingle with your friends and family. I am perfectly capable of walking out of here and finding my car." She started to leave when the sound of his voice stopped her.

Again.

"Tell me one thing."

Scottie turned around slowly. The look in her eyes told him he was on borrowed time. "'One thing,'" she repeated. "I'll hold you to that."

It was obvious that they needed to clear the air if they were to work together. "Why do you react to everything I say to you as if I was either challenging you or trying to reduce you to the status of some kind of mindless rookie? I'm not trying to insult you, or belittle you, or make you feel as if I regard you as anything less than a very capable police detective. One I would like to get to know because, like it or not, as long as we're partners, I expect you to have my back and I damn well intend to have yours. That kind of thing depends on a certain amount of predictability when it comes to one another's actions— and that comes from getting to know one another."

Impatient, Scottie curbed her desire to shift from foot to foot. "Finished?" she asked.

"Yes. For now." The way he said it told her that there would be more later.

"Okay, I'll work on my Bryce Cavanaugh communication skills," Scottie told him. "Will that satisfy you?"

He knew she was being sarcastic, but at least she was aware of the problem and that was a start. "It'll have to," he told her.

"Good. Again, goodbye." She hooked her messenger bag over her shoulder. "I'll see you in the morning." And with that, she began to make her way out of Malone's.

Scottie tried to move swiftly without making any eye contact but that was close to impossible, considering she knew, at least by sight, a number of the people currently gathered in the establishment.

Determined not to exchange any small talk, something she really wasn't very good at, Scottie plowed through the crowd.

Cavanaugh had been right, she thought when she finally reached the front door. This was the place where a lot of the detectives and police officers came at the end of the day.

Opening the heavy oak doors and stepping outside, she took a deep breath. Scottie found that the sun had called it a day, allowing twilight to slip comfortably around the city streets.

She glanced at her watch out of habit. She'd spent less time in Malone's than she'd thought she had. Time had only dragged because she'd been anxious to leave. After being unable to reach Ethan for three days and finding that he hadn't come by the homeless shelter—his one running good deed that he was so proud of—she felt an almost overpowering need to drive by Ethan's apartment, something she normally refrained from doing. Hovering was a habit that took vigilance to keep in check.

Getting into her car, she glanced in the rearview mirror, not just to make sure it was safe to pull out, but also to make sure Cavanaugh hadn't suddenly gotten it into his head to follow her again.

He was nowhere in sight.

Scottie sighed. She was getting paranoid, she told herself.

Okay, so Cavanaugh had initially followed her to the shelter in an attempt to return her phone, but there was something about the man that made her feel that, given half a chance, he would very willingly put himself in charge of her life.

Just like you put yourself in charge of Ethan's? a little voice in her head mocked.

That was different, she silently insisted, pulling out of the parking lot. Ethan was brilliant, far more brilliant than she was, but he really did lack common sense. People in that category were easily taken advantage of. It had already happened to her brother once. Witness the so-called "friends" he had fallen in with several years ago while he was rebelling against everything. Friends who were quick to take advantage of the fact that he could make computers do things that baffled the average computer-savvy users.

They, especially that girl Eva with the multicolored hair, she recalled, manipulated Ethan to do things he would have never done on his own. He'd hacked into computers for the fun of it and then, egged on by those same friends, he'd hacked into other computer systems for the sheer profit of it. Inevitably, he'd been caught. Because he was underage and had no prior record—and she had engaged a top-notch lawyer on his behalf—Ethan had ultimately avoided being sent to prison. But he had done time in juvie.

Once he'd gotten out and she'd made sure that his record was sealed, she'd gotten him a job as a software engineer with a large gaming company and things began looking up. He seemed to have settled in. She had honestly thought that Ethan's life of crime was all behind him.

Maybe it was, she told herself now, driving past a popular strip mall. Maybe all this was a terrible coincidence and Ethan had gone off somewhere for a mini-vacation. Somewhere where he was unable to get a signal on his cell phone.

Even as she told herself that, Scottie sincerely doubted it.

Making a left at a major intersection, she approached Ethan's apartment complex. Her pulse accelerated.

"Damn it, Ethan. You'd better be home, sleeping off a bender. You only get one free get-out-of-jail card. If you've gotten yourself mixed up in something now, I don't know if I'm going to be able to get you out of it."

But wasn't that why she'd transferred departments? To try to stay one jump ahead of whatever was going down with these break-ins and, if he *was* involved, to find a way to hide that?

Her head hurt.

Rather than parking in guest parking, Scottie stopped her car right in front of her brother's first-floor garden apartment door. If he was home, that was all she wanted to know. She wasn't staying.

"Please be home," she murmured under her breath over and over again as she got out of her vehicle.

She rang the bell. When there was no response, she rang it again. And then she knocked, but there was still no response. Sighing, she got back into her car.

But rather than driving off, this time she found a space in guest parking. With her stomach in a knot, she returned to stand in front of Ethan's door.

She gave knocking one more try. Then, stifling the sigh that rose in her chest, she took out the key Ethan had given her. When he had handed her the copy, he'd told her it was his way of proving to her that he had nothing to hide.

She'd never used it before.

Scottie held her breath as she unlocked the door, still fervently hoping she would find her brother sleeping off a drinking spree.

Opening the door, she found the apartment bathed in darkness.

This didn't look good.

Scottie felt around on the wall for the light switch. Turning it on, she looked around. She was in the kitchen. There were dishes stacked in the sink, a testimony to her brother's less than stellar house-keeping. Taking a closer look, she saw that the food looked caked on and was turning colors. That meant he hadn't been here for a while. Maybe even several weeks or so.

Her heart sank further.

"Ethan? Are you home?" she called out, even thought she knew it was hopeless. "It's Scottie."

There was no answer. The sinking feeling consumed her as she carefully made her way through the rest of the apartment.

Ethan was nowhere to be found. While there was no evidence of a scuffle, the apartment looked as if whoever had been there had left in a hurry.

What kind of a hurry and why?

"Damn it, Ethan, what's going on? I'm not supposed to be your keeper anymore. You're almost twenty-four years old," she told the empty bedroom.

Walking to the closet, she saw that there appeared to be nothing missing. No indication that her brother had thrown a handful of clothing into a suitcase for a sudden, impromptu vacation.

Or a getaway.

About to leave the apartment, she doubled back to the kitchen and, on a hunch, opened the refrigerator.

That was when she saw it.

Ethan had left his keys in the refrigerator. From their location, on the bottom shelf, to the left, it looked as if he'd hastily tossed them there just before, she assumed, he'd been dragged away.

That was their signal. Keys in the refrigerator. It was to indicate that something was out of place. Their mother—in her more sober state—had had a habit of misplacing her keys and had left them in the refrigerator more than once.

Scottie took the keys out. They were cold. The

keys had been there for a while. What did that mean? Days? Weeks?

"Okay, so who has you and why?"

She locked up the apartment and stared at the keys in her hand. She needed answers. Someone had to have seen something, although she knew firsthand that witnesses were unreliable. Still, she had to start someplace.

Frustrated, she knocked on the doors of the two neighbors who lived on either side of her brother's apartment.

Starting with the one on the right, she held up her badge when a rather bleary-eyed, barefoot man in a torn blue T-shirt opened the door.

"Something wrong, Officer?"

"Detective," she corrected the man out of habit and then identified herself. "Have you seen your neighbor in 1K lately?"

He shook his head. "I haven't seen anyone," he told her. "I just got in from a double shift and all I want to see is my mattress." The next moment he was closing the door, calling an end to the interview.

She turned to the neighbor who had the apartment to Ethan's left. She rang the bell twice before anyone answered. Again, Scottie identified herself as she held up her badge then asked, "Do you remember when you might have last seen Mr. Loomis?" she asked the woman in the second apartment.

"Who's Mr. Loomis?" the woman asked.

"That would be your neighbor in 1K," Scottie told her patiently.

"I don't butt into people's lives," the woman told her indignantly.

She took measure of the older woman and pressed on, confident that, despite her protest, this *was* a woman who did butt into people's lives whenever possible.

"I didn't mean to imply that you did, but we all notice things as we go about our daily lives," Scottie told her genially. "I just wondered if you'd seen him lately."

The woman sighed, as if thinking, then volunteered, "Not for at least three weeks. The last time I saw him, he was opening his door to let this little skank in."

Alarms instantly went off in Scottie's head. Eva. Ethan's former girlfriend could easily be described that way, especially by someone who was pretending to take the moral high ground.

"Could you describe her to me?" Scottie asked.

"She was a skank," the woman repeated. "She had on a short, tight skirt, a see-through blouse that left nothing to the imagination—this is a respectable apartment complex, you know," the woman interjected indignantly. "There are *kids* here."

Scottie struggled to curb her impatience. "I know, it's shameful. Did you happen to notice if she was a blonde or a brunette? Anything at all you can remember would be helpful," she coaxed.

"She wasn't neither," the woman told her. "The little tramp had blue and green streaks in her hair. Otherwise, it was brown. And she looked like one of those wannabe model types, you know, the ones who eat one grape for lunch and say they're full," the woman complained. "I saw her hanging all over the guy in 1K. Talking to him, touching him. He didn't seem all that into her, but she looked like she had her mind made up about him."

Scottie did her best not to sound as if she was excited. "Did you hear them talking about anything by any chance?" she coaxed.

The woman looked offended. "Are you asking if I eavesdropped?"

"No," Scottie said tactfully, "but if you happened to have heard him call her by her name, that might prove to be very helpful."

Suspicion entered the woman's flat features. "Why are you asking all these questions? Is he some kind of criminal?" Panic entered her voice. "Am I in danger? Should I be asking for police protection?"

"Oh, no, no, nothing like that," Scottie quickly assured the older woman. "Mr. Loomis just hasn't come into work for a few days and his boss asked the police to check this out. He was just worried that something might have happened to him."

"He's probably off partying somewhere with that little bitch," was the woman's guess. "When I saw them, she was carrying this big bottle of whiskey."

Ethan didn't drink. Ever. Seeing what alcohol had done to their mother had made her brother a lifelong member of the temperance league.

"Are you sure?" she asked the woman.

"Of course I'm sure. I know a bottle of whiskey

when I see it. It was one of those pricey brands, you know? Waste of money if you ask me. A cheap bottle does the trick as easily as an expensive one, right? Why all these questions?" the woman asked suspiciously.

"I'm just trying to get all the facts down, that's all, ma'am. And you didn't hear him call her by her name?" Scottie pressed again.

"I already said I didn't, didn't I?" The matronly woman looked over her shoulder into her apartment. "Can I go now? My dinner's getting cold and it just doesn't taste the same if I reheat it," she complained.

"Of course. I'm sorry to have kept you. You've been a great help." That helped placate her brother's neighbor somewhat. Digging into her pocket, Scottie took out one of her cards and held it out to the woman. "Take my card," she coaxed. "This is my phone number, if you happen to remember anything else—anything at all," Scottie stressed. "Please don't hesitate to give me a call."

The woman looked the card over carefully before putting it into her pocket. "Okay, sure. Is there any reward for helping?"

"Just knowing that you did the right thing," Scottie told her.

It was obvious that wasn't what the woman wanted to hear.

"Yeah, a lot that'll get you," the woman grumbled. She closed her door hard.

Scottie hurried back to her car.

Thank God for nosy neighbors, she thought.

Thanks to the gossipy woman she'd just spoken to, she felt that she had a possible lead. It was slim, but right now it was better than nothing and, with any luck, it might actually help lead to her brother.

Because the nosy neighbor had described Ethan's old girlfriend, the one responsible for getting him mixed up with the gang in the first place.

Chapter 6

When Bryce walked into the squad room the next morning, an extra-large container of coffee in his hand, he was mildly surprised to see that his new partner was already there. She appeared to be once again poring through the files that had been compiled for each of the eight previous break-ins.

Sitting, he was able to get only a limited view of Scottie's face. Her head was down because she was reading. She seemed totally oblivious to the fact that he was even there.

She also looked tired, Bryce noted. A great deal more so than she had when she'd left Malone's last night. It made him wonder about the rest of her evening.

Dispensing with the customary "Good morning," he asked, "Rough night, Scottie?"

She raised her eyes for a moment then went back to reading the files. If she was surprised he had come in without her being aware of it, she gave no indication.

"I didn't get much sleep," she murmured, continuing to read.

Bryce took an educated guess. "Insomnia?"

"Something like that." And then, after a moment, she looked up at him. "What made you guess that and not something along the lines of partying too hard and too long?"

That would have been the kind of remark she would have expected him to make, given Cavanaugh's flippant attitude. Granted she'd left Malone's, but there was no reason for him to think she hadn't gotten together with other people instead of going straight home.

Bryce didn't answer immediately, taking a long swig of the coffee he'd brought with him instead. When he set the container down, he told her, "You don't look like the type."

"Meaning I'm dull?"

His new partner really had her back up this morning. "That wouldn't be the word I'd use." A hell of a lot of other words came to mind first, Bryce mused. Like *driven*. One thing he had a gut feeling about, there was nothing dull about the woman sitting opposite him. "You sound like you're spoiling for a fight, Scottie," he observed. "Are you?"

Scottie suppressed a sigh, pushing the file she'd been reading to the center of her desk. So far, nothing had stood out for her, or even waved weakly in passing. "No, all I'm looking for is some peace of mind. I was up all night thinking about these break-ins." Which was true as far as it went. Cavanaugh had no need to know that she was worried about Ethan's possible involvement.

Bryce regarded her over the rim of the container. Definitely driven, he thought. "What about them?"

Scottie put her hand on top of the pile of folders, as if touching them would somehow make what she was looking for apparent to her. Her eyes met his. "I'm trying to find what the common thread is here."

Bryce laughed dryly. "*That* is the million-dollar question and, so far, nobody's come up with an answer—other than all the houses that were broken into were located in Aurora—and all the break-ins were clean, without any signs of forced entry. I suspect that's why the lieutenant wanted a fresh pair of eyes to go over all the files." His description replayed itself in his head as he looked at her again. "Right now, if you don't mind my saying so, your eyes don't look very fresh."

Scottie frowned at his observation. She didn't want Cavanaugh getting personal in any way. She didn't have time for it and, more importantly, if he did succeed in getting close to her, there was more than a fifty-fifty chance he'd eventually find out about Ethan.

Under normal circumstances, that wouldn't matter to her. But given that she thought her brother was somehow involved in these break-ins—now more than ever since she'd talked to his nosy neighbor—she definitely didn't want Cavanaugh finding out about Ethan.

The best way to keep him out of her life was to be off-putting, so she said, "Actually, yes, I do mind you saying that."

Bryce pulled over a pad and began to write. As he wrote, he gave voice to what he was writing down. "New partner is sensitive and not in a good way."

That definitely caught her attention—as well as irritated her. "What are you doing?" she asked.

He looked up, a far too likable grin on his face.

Just what was his game? Scottie wondered.

"Putting together a list of your traits," he told her. "I figured that since you seem to be against letting us get to know one another the traditional way—by talking—I have to resort to making a list from my own observations. You know, like any good detective."

"A good detective doesn't waste time like this, getting distracted by trivial things," she informed him tersely.

"I'm afraid that I can't help myself." His smile went up a notch. "You really are so damn distracting," he told her.

The lines were dumb, Scottie thought, but there was something almost magnetic about that smile of his.

Focus, Scottie! she ordered herself.

"Do you just come up with these lines at will,"

she asked him, "or do you stay up nights, compiling them?"

He pretended to be hurt by the remark. "That was cold, Scottie."

"What's going to be cold is the trail that these break-in artists left behind if you don't stop wasting time trying to get a handle on me," she informed him. "What we need to get a handle on is them."

There was that smile again, half magnetic, half wicked, and almost next to impossible to block out, she thought, exasperated.

"I've always been able to multitask, Scottie." He looked at her innocently. "Haven't you?"

In addition to trying to ignore that grin of his, she was grappling with a steadily growing feeling of urgency that something awful was going to happen if she didn't find these thieves before it was too late. Playing word games with Cavanaugh was a definite hindrance.

"Tell you what," she told him. "We put in a full day working these break-ins and, at the end, you can play two questions."

"The name of the game is Twenty Questions," Bryce corrected.

She wasn't about to go that far. "My game, my rules," Scottie informed him. "You get to ask me two questions, take it or leave it."

"And you'll answer them?" he asked skeptically.

"Yes." She wouldn't be happy about it, but she would do what she had to do to protect Ethan. If that meant allowing Cavanaugh to get closer to her—at least partially—so be it.

His eyes held hers. "Truthfully?"

She pressed her lips together. The man was annoyingly intuitive. "Yes," she snapped.

He grinned broadly. "Okay, let's go."

"You do realize that you're getting paid to do what I just bribed you into doing," Scottie pointed out.

He appeared almost boyish as he answered. "Yeah, I know." Time to get down to work, Bryce thought, finishing his coffee. "Okay, Person With Fresh Eyes, how do you want to go about this?"

She took the simplest route. "I'd like to interview the victims again, see if anything new comes to light," Scottie told him.

Bryce had taken the case over from another detective, who had since retired, so he hadn't conducted the initial interviews with the first four break-in victims. Her idea had merit. "In other words, start from the beginning."

"Yes." She expected him to veto the idea or at least to give her some resistance about it. She was prepared to be insistent. So she was rather surprised when Cavanaugh said, "All right, then let's get started."

This was too easy. He was going to come up with some kind of conditions he wanted met first, she thought. "You're not going to argue with me about it?"

"Should I?" he asked.

"No, of course not, but—"

In the interests of getting started—and not torturing her any further—Bryce cut her off. "Well, then it's nice to know I'm measuring up to your expectations." Circumventing his desk, he came around to hers and then, leaning over her, pulled out the oldest case from the bottom of the pile. "According to the report that was filed, the Taylors were the first victims. We can go question them first," he proposed.

Turning her chair, she wound up looking right up at him. She was closer than she was happy about, but she had nowhere to back up to. "'We'?" she repeated. "You want to come with me?"

Did she think he was just going to send her off? "We're working the case together, aren't we?" It was more of a statement than a question.

"Yes, but I just assumed there'd be a division of labor. I'd question the victims while you…worked on other possible leads," she tagged on.

Cavanaugh was smiling at her, the kind of smile that belonged on the face of an indulgent parent. That and having him standing closer to her than her shadow did nothing for her frame of mind.

"What?" Scottie all but demanded.

There was no way he was letting her off on her own. He still had no idea just what sort of a detective she was and since this was his case, he was responsible for it—and, in a way, for her.

Still, he knew if he said anything of the sort, he'd have a problem on his hands. So, instead, he decided to appeal to her common sense.

"Ever hear that old saying about two heads being better than one?" he asked.

"What about it?" Her tone was wary.

"Well," he went on to point out needlessly, "each of those heads has a set of ears."

She was still waiting, but she was also resigning herself to being teamed up with Cavanaugh. She would have to be careful with her questions, she thought.

She conceded. "No argument."

His grin grew wider. "Finally," he couldn't resist saying. "Anyway," he quickly continued, "one of us might hear something the other doesn't when we question the victims again. Sometimes, the slightest thing could lead to solving the crime."

He wasn't saying anything she hadn't already thought on her own. She'd resisted the idea of having Cavanaugh come with her when she questioned the victims because having him there would make her feel hemmed in and constricted. She wouldn't be able to show any of the victims Ethan's picture to see if they'd seen him in the vicinity—not without having her partner start asking her questions.

But there was no way she could protest having him along without possibly arousing his suspicions. "You're right," she told him. To her amazement, he began to write on his pad again. "Now what?" she demanded.

"'New partner can be fair and is willing to concede arguments,'" he read out loud, putting down his pen.

"Are you going to keep doing that?" she demanded.

"Only when you blow me away," he told her. He meant it as a compliment. She wasn't taking it as such.

Instead her eyes narrowed as she glared at him. "Don't tempt me," she muttered under her breath only to have him laugh.

"I heard that," he told her, amusement playing over his chiseled features.

"Then you also heard that I said you could ask me two questions at the end of the day, so put that damn pad away," she ordered. "Or that offer I just made will be null and void."

"Your wish is my command," Bryce quipped, dropping the yellow, ruled pad into his center drawer and then closing the drawer.

Scottie glanced at him one more time before they headed out. "If only," she replied only to hear his resonant, full-bodied laugh in response.

Taking the first three folders with him, Bryce led the way to the elevator.

"By the way," he said, pressing the down button for the elevator, "your presence created quite a stir at Malone's last night. My brothers came up to me after you left and wanted to know what I had on you."

"'Had on me'?" she repeated, not certain just what he was implying.

"Yeah. They thought I had stumbled across some dire secret of yours that I threatened to make public unless you came to Malone's with me. They didn't think anything else would make you come."

Granted she had never set foot in the popular hangout before, but she hadn't thought anyone had noticed. She wondered if Cavanaugh was just pulling her leg now. "You people have nothing better to do than talk about why I came to Malone's?" she asked incredulously.

"Cops always have something to talk about," he reminded her. "The whole point in unwinding is having something inconsequential to talk about so that the heavy-duty subjects get put on hold for a little while. You know that." He looked at his partner as they got on the elevator. Maybe Scottie had a different sort of escape mechanism. "Don't you?" he questioned.

She shrugged, dismissing the subject. "I don't kick back."

He wasn't sure if he believed her. But just in case she was telling him the truth, he said, "Well, that's going to have to change."

What gave him the right to think he could just come in and reorchestrate her life just because she was working with him? "And just why is that?"

He would have thought the answer was obvious to her. "Because if you don't kick back, you'll self-destruct. I've seen it more than once. If you're going to be my partner—and it looks like you are—I'd like you to last for a while."

Several retorts rose to her lips, but all of them would just lead to arguments so she forced herself to say, "We'll see."

Right now she needed Cavanaugh, for cover, if

for no other reason. She needed to remain in Robbery until she satisfied herself that her brother was just being thoughtless and immature—which at the moment was the best-case scenario she could come up with.

She didn't want to think about worse case.

"Yeah, we will," Bryce agreed. "By the way," he went on as they got off the elevator and headed for the rear exit, "I'll drive."

She didn't care about driving one way or another—or thought she didn't until he had made that declaration. And then she felt her back going up. She'd been in charge for so long, she didn't know how to take orders without feeling as if she was being slighted.

"Why you?" she asked.

Was she serious? he wondered. "Because I'd need a shoehorn to get into your car and because I've seen the way you drive and I'd like to live long enough to know if I'm going to be an uncle or an aunt," he said as he led the way to his car.

She quickened her pace to keep up. "Come again?"

"Just my way of trying to lighten the mood," he told her. "I was referring to finding out whether Duncan's wife is going to give birth to a girl or a boy."

She vaguely remembered the conversation at Malone's last night. Right now, her attention was focused on what he'd just said a minute ago. "What's wrong with the way I drive?" she asked.

"Nothing if you're driving the getaway car after a high-stakes bank robbery," he told her.

Meaning he thought she drove too fast, Scottie thought. She took offense at that. She only drove as fast as it seemed safe. "You're exaggerating," she informed him coolly.

"For once, no, I'm not," he told her with finality. And then, for the sake of the fledgling partnership and because he wasn't the type to walk all over someone's feelings unless absolutely necessary, he said, "Okay, how's this for a reason? Because I'm lead detective on the case."

Scottie shrugged. In her experience, most lead detectives preferred to be driven than drive.

"Still not a good reason," she informed him, getting in on the passenger side of his vehicle, "but have it your way."

"Thanks." Bryce said the lone word with feeling, as if they were having a regular conversation and he was actually thanking her for something. He went so far as to put the key into the ignition and then he turned to her to ask, "You went through the files yesterday, right?"

Why was he asking her that? He'd given her the files and he'd seen her go through them. For the sake of harmony and not coming across any more combative than he probably already thought of her, Scottie refrained from saying as much and instead just said, "Right."

"Any thoughts?"

The question struck her as rather vague. "About who did it?"

He started up his vehicle and pulled out of the

parking spot. "About any of it. Anything you read stick out, in your opinion?"

She did a quick review of what she'd read. "The break-ins all occurred around the same time of day. They all occurred when there was no one home. And they all occurred in houses that were located in the upscale area of Aurora."

And considering that all the neighborhoods in the city were deemed to be upper-middle class, that was saying a lot.

"Anything else?" he asked her.

Scottie looked at him. By his tone, she knew there *was* something else but she was temporarily drawing a blank. "Should there be?"

"They all had insurance."

Where was he going with this? "You think there was collusion?" she asked.

"Could be something to explore," Bryce suggested.

She looked at his profile in silence for a long moment.

Feeling her eyes on him, it was his turn to ask, "What?"

"I guess you're not just another pretty face, after all," she deadpanned.

She was rewarded with the sound of his rich laughter. She hated to admit it, but it really did have a nice sound.

"I think we're having our first moment, Scottie," he told her, amused as well as relieved to discover that she did have a sense of humor.

"If you say so," she replied.

He glanced at her then back to the road. The impression of his smile lasted awhile in her mind's eye.

"I say so," he acknowledged.

Scottie did her best to block out his presence as well as his smile. She had a string of break-ins to solve—and a wayward brother to possibly save. There was no room for a devastatingly handsome detective in that mix.

Chapter 7

"I suppose you're going to want to ask all the questions," Scottie said as they approached their first break-in victims' house, an impressive-looking, custom-made home.

"No, we can take turns," Bryce told her. "But I'll start," he said as he took out his ID and rang the doorbell.

Scottie followed suit, taking out hers just as the front door opened.

An average looking man in his late fifties stood in the doorway. He eyed them a bit warily. "Yes?"

"Detectives Cavanaugh and Scott, sir," Bryce said, introducing himself and Scottie. "We'd like to ask you a few questions regarding the recent break-in you experienced."

"Don't you people talk to each other?" Donald Taylor asked irritably as he looked from one ID to the other. "I already gave my statement to the police officer who responded to our call. And to the detective he called in. *And* to the insurance company, so we could eventually be reimbursed. Frankly, I'm tired of talking about it." He continued to hold the door ajar. "Myra and I just want to put the whole thing behind us."

Bryce put his foot in the doorway to keep the man from closing the door on them.

"We understand that, sir," he told the software CEO, "but you might have heard in the news that yours was apparently the first in a series of break-ins occurring in Aurora."

The expression on the man's face said he found that piece of information annoying, as well. "Yes, I heard. You people are really having trouble doing your job, aren't you?" he scoffed.

"Which is why we'd like your help," Scottie put in before the exchange devolved into an altercation of heated words.

A mild interest flickered in the break-in victim's eyes as he looked in her direction. "I can't see what I can do," he told the two detectives.

"If you could just go over everything one more time, something might come to light that was overlooked before," Bryce suggested patiently.

It was obvious that the theft victim's back went up. "You think I'm hiding something?" the man demanded angrily.

"No," Scottie assured him soothingly. "It's just that things come back to us at different intervals. You might remember something now that you didn't when you were first giving your statement."

Taylor frowned, thinking her words over. "Sounds reasonable, I guess."

"Stop being so antagonistic, Donald. They're only trying to do their job," his wife admonished, sweeping into the foyer and drawing the door open. "Please, won't you come in?" the woman invited. "My husband's used to people cowering at the sound of his voice. Donald forgets that not everyone works for him." She gave her husband a withering look then beckoned the detectives into the house.

Myra Taylor led them into a tastefully—and expensively—decorated living room with eighteen-foot vaulted ceilings. Taking a seat on a wide sectional, she indicated the love seat opposite it.

"So," Mrs. Taylor said, settling in, "how can we help?"

"Is this going to get my coin collection back?" Taylor wanted to know before another word was uttered. "The insurance claim adjuster said they'd be cutting a check to cover my loss but there's no way that money is going to begin to cover it," he complained adamantly.

"Donald's a coin collector from way back," his wife confided. It was easy to see she didn't share her husband's enthusiasm about the collection. "He liked telling everyone about them. Showed them off at the drop of a hat." She frowned disapprovingly. "I knew it would only be a matter of time before someone tried to steal them," she declared knowingly.

"They didn't just *try*," her husband snapped, irritated. "They succeeded."

Not wanting this to turn into a family argument, Bryce quickly stepped in.

"Why don't you walk us through that day?" he suggested. "And then, if you wouldn't mind, we'd like a list of what was taken."

Taylor's irritation grew. "I already gave that to the insurance company," he protested.

"I made a copy," Myra cheerfully volunteered, getting up. "I can get it now."

Bryce stopped her by assuring the woman, "After we go over the events of that day will be fine, Mrs. Taylor."

In quick, staccato sentences, Taylor went over coming home from a meeting in the late afternoon the day of the break-in and not realizing at first that anything had been taken.

"I noticed that the back door wasn't locked," Myra spoke up.

Her husband shot her an annoyed look. "Yeah, after *we* saw that, I decided to check the safe in the master bedroom to see if anything was taken." His scowl intensified. "Everything in there was gone."

"Everything?" Bryce questioned. "Could you be a little more specific?"

"Yeah, coins, jewelry, cash. *Everything*," Taylor emphasized grudgingly.

Scottie wondered if the house had been deliberately targeted. If Taylor had bragged about his coin collection, he might have also mentioned that he kept cash in the safe, as well.

"How much cash?" she asked.

His wife spoke up before Taylor could answer the question. "Fifty thousand dollars."

The amount sounded a little excessive, Bryce thought. "Do you usually keep that much available cash in the house?"

"It wasn't 'in the house,' it was in the safe," Taylor corrected. "And, yes, I do. I like to feel that if anything unexpected comes up, I can deal with it."

And how many people did he tell that to, Bryce wondered. That would definitely tempt a lot of cash-strapped people. "You said you had home insurance?"

"Yes, mainly for my jewelry," Myra interjected, "but it covered the coin collection, too."

"Not really," Taylor grumbled. "There were pieces in the collection that were irreplaceable—and priceless as far as I was concerned," he declared sullenly.

"We're going to try to get your collection back for you, Mr. Taylor, as well as your jewelry, Mrs. Taylor," Scottie told the couple. "Now we just have a few more questions—"

Mrs. Taylor looked far more cooperative than her husband. "Ask away," she urged.

Getting answers to the "few more questions" took longer than either Scottie or her new partner expected. Consequently it seemed like hours before they were able to finally take their leave of the couple.

Tired before, Scottie felt definitely drained as she and Bryce drove away from the three-story, custom-designed home.

Bryce blew out a breath as they put distance between themselves and the victims. "Well, that's definite proof that money doesn't buy happiness," he commented. Glancing in Scottie's direction, he asked, "Want to stop for lunch?"

"What I want is to go question the second victim," she told him.

He didn't feel he'd learned anything new questioning the Taylors, but that didn't mean talking to the victims was a waste of time. Obviously, Scottie seemed to think it was worthwhile.

"The number's in the file," he told her. "Call and see if he's home."

"Apparently he's not," she told Bryce after her third attempt to reach victim number two went to voice mail. With a sigh, she put away her cell phone.

"Now can we go get something to eat, or do you want to jump to victim number three?" Bryce asked.

She didn't want Cavanaugh to think she was being unduly obsessed with the break-ins. He might find that suspect, so she switched gears.

"Are you one of those people who gets grumpy if he's not fed regularly?" she asked him.

Rather than answer her, Bryce asked a question of his own. "Is that a personal question, Detective

Scott? I'm not sure if I can answer that in light of our previous arrangement."

Maybe she had that coming, Scottie thought. "I said I didn't want to share my personal life. You can share yours to your heart's content."

"Well, that seems rather one-sided," Bryce commented. "Lucky thing for you, I don't take offense easily."

"Lucky," she echoed. Looking down at the files on her lap, she made a quick decision. "Okay, let's get lunch and pick this up again later."

She was rewarded by a broad smile. "Sounds good to me. What are you in the mood for?" he asked.

Scottie never hesitated. "Answers."

"I was talking about lunch," Bryce pointed out.

She shrugged indifferently. Food was food to her. "Whatever you want," she told him.

"You don't have any preferences?" he asked incredulously.

"Nope. Whatever's close by is fine with me," she answered.

That surprised him. If asked, he would have guessed that his new partner had a particular list of things she ate and things she rejected. Maybe he'd misread her, Bryce thought.

"How about Chinese?" he questioned, waiting to see if she would actually go along with his choice.

"Sure. Why not?" she told him gamely.

"I know just the place."

She nodded, slipping the top file back into her messenger bag. "I figured you would," she told him.

As Bryce drove to the closest storefront restaurant he knew that specialized in decent Chinese food, he spared his partner a glance. Unlike his old partner, Scottie didn't talk much. Right now, she seemed to be intently studying the list of stolen goods they'd gotten from Taylor's wife.

"What's so interesting?" he asked.

"I don't know yet," she replied.

That was a lie, really. Her attention was focused on Taylor's stolen coin collection. Growing up, her brother's prize possession—his *only* possession, really, was a very small coin collection he had put together by carefully culling early dated coins out of circulation. He would take a roll of nickels to the bank and exchange them for another roll of nickels, which he would take home, open up and search through for an early dated coin. When he found one, it was like Christmas for him, she recalled. What captured his fascination was not just the coin itself, but who had had the coin before him.

When he had finally landed a job with the gaming company, putting his life together, she'd given him a special set of uncirculated Walking Liberty half dollars. His eyes had shone.

Was this Ethan's handiwork, after all? If it was, she was certain he hadn't pulled it off alone, but it did seem to have his fingerprints all over it. At least figuratively.

She was reading things into this, Scottie reproached herself. One clue at a time. She needed to take this slow to see where it ultimately ended up taking her.

It took Scottie a minute to realize that the car was no longer moving. Cavanaugh had pulled up into a parking lot and was just sitting there, looking at her.

She was slipping. She was usually far more aware of her surroundings than this. This thing with Ethan had really thrown her. She needed to get hold of herself, otherwise, she wasn't going to do herself, or Ethan, any good.

"You're not driving," she noted.

"Nothing gets by you, does it?" Bryce commented, amused. "I'm not driving because we're here. At the restaurant," he added when she didn't seem to pick up what he was telling her. "Would you like to get out of the vehicle?" he suggested.

"Oh, right."

Not wanting to take a chance with leaving the folders in the car, she quickly slipped the folders back into her messenger bag.

Holding the restaurant door open for her, Bryce waited until she entered the crowded restaurant then walked in behind her.

"You looked as if you were really absorbing everything in the folder, not to mention memorizing the list Taylor gave us. So, got any thoughts about the break-ins?"

"They were methodical, precise and done by someone who knew what he or she was doing." There was more, but she was still working that out in her head and wasn't ready to share it with him.

"You think it was just one person involved?" he questioned. Catching the hostess's eye, he held up two fingers. The woman grabbed two menus and beckoned them forward.

Scottie shook her head in response to his question. "Most likely not. I get the impression that there's at least two, maybe three, people involved." Ethan's old gang was comprised of four other people—and him. Each had a particular skill.

Bryce resisted the temptation to put his hand to her back to usher her along as they followed the hostess to a free table. "Go on."

"I think one person decides which houses to break into."

His head filled with questions. "What's their criteria? How do they know which houses to break into and how do they know when?"

She could tell him what she really thought, but that could very well implicate Ethan. So, for now, she came up with alternate theories in hopes of leading Bryce astray until she worked things out to her own satisfaction.

Sitting at the table, she said, "I suppose that there could be someone watching them. According to the résumés we've got on the victims, these are not your run-of-the-mill nine-to-fivers. These are CEOs, trust fund babies, self-made millionaires. They don't hold down regular jobs and yet, so far, not a single one of them was home when the break-ins occurred."

"'Watching them,'" Bryce repeated. "You mean like tailing them?"

She shook her head. She knew she could say yes and she and her partner could waste a lot of time collecting various traffic cam videos from all points surrounding the houses that had suffered break-ins, but she didn't want to insult Cavanaugh's intelligence. She was fairly certain he'd see right through that quickly enough.

"No. Looking over their statements, none of the victims mentioned that they felt someone was following them, so I don't think there was any actual 'physical' tailing involved."

The waiter came by and Bryce gave his order mechanically. He ordered the same thing every time. His philosophy was, if something worked, don't mess with it. He expected Scottie to pause and peruse the menu but she surprised him by telling the server, "Lobster Cantonese, two egg rolls," and then handed the menu to him.

"You think that whoever put in their security monitor might be involved?" Bryce asked her as soon as the server left.

"That was the first thing I went over," she told him. "All the victims have different security systems, installed by different people." She paused to allow that to sink in. "But that doesn't mean that one person can't hack into those different systems and disarm them."

Bryce looked at her. She was onto something, he thought. He could tell by the look in her eyes. But he had the feeling she wasn't about to share that piece of information, either, not until she was fairly certain about it.

"Why don't we question some more of the victims," Scottie said, "and I'll keep going over their lists of missing items as well as what they tell us. Maybe we'll see a pattern."

Bryce raised his eyes to hers and she couldn't read his expression. All she knew was that he made her want to squirm—for more than one reason.

"You see a pattern already, don't you?" he asked quietly.

She wanted to say no, but she had a feeling he wouldn't believe her, so she resorted to a half lie. "I'm not sure yet."

The truth of it was, she was looking for another explanation. Her brother couldn't be the only computer genius around who had the ability to hack into computers and security systems. There had to be others who could do what he did, right? Maybe this was the work of someone else who knew how to get computers to do what they needed done.

She was retreating, Bryce thought. He needed to get her to trust him and to keep advancing this case until they caught whoever was behind all this. "Well, you tell me what you need and we'll go from there."

She wanted to stall.

Now that she felt she was actually onto something, she had a queasy feeling in the pit of her stomach and she wanted to step back and search for another explanation—and pray that Ethan had come to his senses. He knew what finding out that he was involved in this would cost her, knew what side of the law he was supposed to be on. Would he just throw everything away this way?

If it *was* him, she had to believe he was doing this unwillingly. Otherwise, she didn't think she could bear it.

"You look like something's on your mind," Bryce commented.

Damn, she was going to have to work on her poker face. "Lunch," she told him, looking around for the server to return with their orders.

"No, something else," he told her.

She shrugged. "I don't like people who steal things from other people. I grew up poor and all I ever wanted was to be able to earn enough money to buy the things I wanted."

The expression in his eyes told her he knew it was more than that but because their partnership was in its infancy, for now he didn't push.

But she had a feeling that he would eventually. And soon.

Please get your act together, Ethan. And soon, she prayed.

Chapter 8

"By the way, that qualifies," she informed him as she bit into her egg roll.

Bryce looked at her, confused. The remark had come out of nowhere. "Come again?"

"We made a bargain earlier," Scottie reminded him. "I said I'd share two personal things about myself with you at the end of the day. Well, it's not the end of the day yet, but what I just told you qualifies as a personal fact, so that's 'one.'"

Bryce was well aware that she had pulled back the curtain a tiny bit and showed him something from her private life. He nodded, smiling at her. "I wasn't going to say anything because I thought maybe you were on a roll and would just go on opening up."

A faint smile curved the corners of her mouth. "Nope."

Bryce decided that maybe a little one-for-one trade might be in order. "Anything about me you want to know?" he asked.

"Nope."

He believed her. That made her pretty unique in his book. "A woman devoid of curiosity. You are a rare creature, Alexandra Scott."

She had a feeling he was trying to trick her into lowering her guard. "You're not going to flatter me into opening up."

Bryce laughed to himself. "Didn't think so." He was almost finished with his chicken lo mein when his cell phone began to pulse. Setting his chopsticks down, he took his phone out of his pocket. "Cavanaugh."

The next moment, as Scottie looked in his direction, she saw his expression change. Had there been another break-in?

"Slow down," he urged the person on the other end of the call. "Where are you?"

Maybe it wasn't another break-in, but there was something definitely wrong. Scottie stopped eating. She heard the concern in her partner's voice and did her best to try to fill in the blanks.

"I'll be right there." Terminating the call, Bryce tucked his cell back in his pocket. "We've got to go," he told Scottie.

She picked up her messenger bag. "I kind of figured that part out. Who called? Was there another break-in?" she asked.

Bryce looked around for their server. "That was Noelle."

The name meant nothing to her and she waited for Bryce to explain further. But he was waving over the server. As soon as the latter drew closer, Bryce said, "I need the check and a couple of to-go containers along with two bags."

The server nodded. It was obvious from their initial interaction that the man knew who Bryce was. "Urgent police business, Detective?"

"Something like that," Bryce said. He took out a couple of twenties and handed them to the server. "This should cover the bill."

Scottie started to open her bag. "I can pay my own way," she protested.

Bryce waved away her attempt to give him money. "Don't worry, I have a feeling that you will."

Scottie had no idea what he was talking about. "What's that supposed to mean? And who's Noelle?" she asked.

"My brother Duncan's wife," he told her as the server hurried over with the containers he'd requested. The man quickly deposited what was left of their lunches into them. "My brother Duncan's very pregnant wife," Bryce emphasized.

Now she recalled the exchange between her partner and his brother at Malone's last night. Bryce looked worried, she thought. "Is there something wrong?"

"Yeah. She's stuck in traffic and she can't reach Duncan."

"Okay." She still didn't understand why his sister-in-law had called Bryce.

Nodding at the server, Bryce took his doggie bag. "And her water broke half an hour ago."

"Oh." Now it made sense. Scottie grabbed her own doggie bag and headed for the door. "Let's go. You drive and I'll keep trying to get Duncan," she volunteered.

Given the way she claimed to feel about keeping their private lives separate from their work lives, Bryce had half expected his partner to hang back or suggest calling in paramedics rather than going to Noelle with him. Instead he found he had to hurry to catch up to her.

"You are full of surprises, Scottie," he told her, following her out the door.

She didn't understand why he would say that. "Why? Because I want to help a pregnant woman in labor?"

Reaching the car, Scottie got in on the passenger side. She put her doggie bag on the floor and buckled up.

"It's not exactly part of the actual job definition, especially not for a detective," he pointed out, getting in behind the wheel. Because there was no room on his side, he deposited his doggie bag next to hers on the floor on Scottie's side.

"Oh, I don't know," she contradicted. "This is the 'serve' part of protect and serve."

He made his way out of the parking lot. Traffic, he noted, seemed rather heavy for this time of day. It was past lunchtime. "Yeah, I guess you could look at it that way."

She dug her phone out of her bag. "What's your brother's cell number?" she asked. Bryce rattled off the number. She quickly entered it on the keypad. The call connected, then immediately devolved into static.

"Did you get him?" Bryce asked. He was doing his best to change lanes but each lane seemed to be moving slower than the last.

"No, just static. They must be working on one of the cell towers in the area," she commented, terminating the call and trying again.

"Keep trying."

"That's what I'm doing," she told him. Her second attempt had the same results as her first. Nothing but static. She tried one more time then closed her phone, deciding to wait a few minutes.

"No luck?" Bryce asked, glancing at her.

"No luck. I'll try again in a few minutes. Was there an accident?" she asked. "There's an awful lot of traffic for this time of day."

"Yeah, I know," he said impatiently.

She decided not to press. There was nothing either of them could do about the traffic. She waited for it to clear up.

As they went down one of the longer blocks, they saw what the problem was. It looked as if some sort of glitch had shut down the power grid, causing traffic lights to go out for what looked like at least a mile in either direction.

"We could make better time getting to Noelle if we got out and walked," Bryce complained, craning his neck to see how far the problem went.

He appeared genuinely concerned and she gave him points for that. Maybe he wasn't all ego, sexy smile and great hair. "You sure you know the location of her car?" she asked Bryce.

He nodded. She could see he was gripping the steering wheel hard in his frustration. "She said she was stuck just past the intersection of Jefferson Road and Alton."

"That's not that far from here," Scottie said. "Although, given the way this traffic is moving, it might as well be in the next city."

"I know," he grumbled. "When she couldn't reach Duncan, she decided to drive herself to the hospital—before she got stuck in traffic. Move!" he shouted in frustration at the cars in front of him. "Maybe we *should* get out and walk."

Scottie had a better idea. "Drive on the sidewalk," she told him.

Bryce looked at her as if she'd lost her mind. "What?"

"Drive on the sidewalk," she repeated. Because of the drought, the city had allowed most of the grass to die a natural death so there wasn't anything to really damage along the sidewalks. "It's the only way we're going to be able to get to your sister-in-law sooner than later. Driving is still preferable to running."

He weighed his options. "You used to watch those over-the-top action movies as a kid, didn't you?" he guessed.

Not waiting for an answer, Bryce maneuvered his vehicle to the right and drove it onto a long stretch of sidewalk as stunned drivers watched.

Scottie reached over and flipped on the portable siren and whirling lights. "As a matter of fact, I did. That's two," she told him.

He kept his eyes on the sidewalk, looking out for pedestrians. "Two?"

"Two personal facts about me," she told him. "That's all you get." Sticking her head out the passenger-side window, she waved her hand urgently and called out, "Get out of the way!" to a man who seemed oblivious to his surroundings as he walked his miniature greyhound. "This is an emergency!" she shouted. The man retreated, yanking his dog along with him.

Scottie sank back in her seat with a relieved sigh. "What color is Noelle's car?" she asked, realizing she had no idea what kind of car she was looking for.

"She's driving a '05 Scion," he told her. "It's olive green."

"Not exactly a showstopper," Scottie commented. For the most part, the road was filled with black, white and silver vehicles. "At least that's in our favor. Shouldn't be hard to spot." The words were no sooner out of her mouth than she thought she saw the vehicle her partner had just described. "There. I see it," she announced excitedly, pointing ahead. "She's right in the middle lane. Step on it," she ordered.

"You would've made a great drill sergeant," he said, pressing down on the accelerator.

Several minutes later, still traveling on the sidewalk, Bryce was parallel to his sister-in-law's vehicle. The moment he was, Scottie surprised him by getting out and running over to the olive green Scion.

Turning off the ignition, Bryce got out on his side. "Wait up, damn it!" he called after her.

Scottie was knocking on the passenger side of the Scion. When Noelle looked in her direction, Scottie saw that the woman was perspiring heavily. Scottie jerked her thumb up, indicating that she needed to unlock the doors.

Looking as if she was in the throes of excruciating pain, Noelle felt around on the armrest next to her until she found the lock release button, then pressed down on it. The locks popped up. Scottie pulled open the passenger door just as Bryce came up behind her.

Recognition flooded Noelle's face. "Oh, thank God," she cried. "Bryce, I think…the baby's…coming. Did…you…reach Duncan?"

"No, I couldn't get through." He looked over his shoulder. If he continued driving on the sidewalk, he could get his sister-in-law to the hospital. "C'mon, let me help you out of there, Noelle. We can drive you to the hospital."

But as Bryce leaned in from the passenger side, ready to slide his sister-in-law over, Noelle cried out in pain. He pulled back, concerned. "Did I hurt you?"

"No... There's...no...time. The baby's...coming," Noelle cried just short of a scream.

Bryce felt a wave of panic wash over him. He'd been hoping to get Noelle to the hospital before it got to this point. "Now?"

"Now!" Noelle cried, biting down on her lower lip to keep from screaming.

Scottie moved her partner back. "Help me get her into the backseat," she told Bryce. "She needs to lie down and there's not enough room in the front to do what needs to be done."

Bryce looked at her. "You know what you're doing?" he asked.

"Praying mostly," she answered. "C'mon, let's do this."

Scottie crawled through the backseat, opening the door and waiting until Bryce picked up his sister-in-law. As gently as he could, he deposited Noelle in the back of her Scion.

"Hang on, Noelle, I'm going to pull you back so you can lie down," Scottie told her as she laced her arms around Noelle just below the pregnant woman's breasts.

"Okay," Noelle panted, doing her best not to cry out as she was pulled along the seat.

Once Noelle was lying down, Bryce looked at his partner. "Have you done this before?" he asked. "Because I haven't."

"We both had training, right?" Scottie reminded her partner. Every police officer was taught the rudimentary steps involved in helping a woman give birth—then hoped never to be faced with that situation.

Taking a look at Bryce's face, Scottie made a judgment call. "Switch places with me," she told him. "And while you're at it, go get the takeout bags out of your car."

He stared at her, dumbfounded. "You're going to eat at a time like this?"

"I saw the server throw in packets of moist towelettes into the bags," she told him. "It wouldn't hurt to wipe my hands."

Bryce hurried to get the bags as Scottie got in the backseat to take his place.

Looking down at Bryce's sister-in-law, she saw the pain and fear in Noelle's face. She knew it wasn't possible to make her comfortable, but she tried to put the woman at ease, at least a little.

"Hi, we haven't been introduced. My name's Alexandra Scott. I'm your brother-in-law's new partner."

"Duncan…told…me…he…met *you*!" Noelle cried.

"Is this your first baby?" Scottie asked, trying to find something to get the other woman's mind off her pain.

"No…my…second," Noelle answered, breathing really hard.

Scottie smiled at the woman, searching for something to say. "They say the second one's easier."

"They…*lied*!" Noelle cried out, arching her back to the point that she nearly tumbled sideways off the seat.

"Here, this what you want?" Bryce asked, handing her all the packets of wipes he'd found in the bag.

"Yes." Taking one of the packets, Scottie ripped it open with her teeth. Taking out the small, folded wipe, she unfolded it and quickly passed it over her hands, then dropped it on the floor.

"How far apart are your contractions?" she asked Noelle.

"They're...*not*," Noelle cried, fisting her hands on either side of her as she arched her back again, trying to rise above the pain.

"Okay, that's good," Scottie told her, doing her best to sound encouraging. "That means you're almost home free." She turned toward Bryce. "Get in on the other side of the car and prop Noelle up so she can push better when I tell her to," she instructed.

This whole thing felt surreal to him. "She's going to push?" he heard himself asking numbly.

She sympathized with him. There were a million other places she knew he would have rather been. He wasn't the only one, she thought.

"I don't think the baby's ready to waltz out on its own, so, yes, Noelle's going to push. Move," she ordered, snapping Bryce out of the momentary trance he was in.

Coming to, Bryce hurried around the vehicle and got in on the other side of his sister-in-law. He saw that Scottie had already folded back Noelle's dress and made her as ready as possible. Getting right behind her, he raised Noelle's shoulders slightly, keeping her at an angle. Suddenly he felt her going rigid.

"Scottie?" he questioned, looking up at his partner.

Scottie's attention was completely focused on the woman about to give birth. "Okay, Noelle, you look pretty dilated," Scottie told her. "I guess this is showtime. Ready?" It was a rhetorical question. "Push!"

Noelle did as she was ordered while Scottie counted up to sixty under her breath. When she reached it, she ordered, "Okay, stop pushing!"

"Why?" Noelle panted. "Is…the…baby…here?"

"No, not yet." In her own way, she felt as exhausted as Noelle did. Waiting, Scottie counted up to sixty again, this time silently. When she reached sixty, she said, "Okay, Cavanaugh, prop her up again," she told him. Smiling at Noelle, she said, "You know the drill, Noelle. Push!"

Grunts and cries of anguish accompanied Noelle's pushing. So much so that she barely heard Scottie cry, "Stop!"

When the order registered, Noelle collapsed against Bryce, who drew back just enough to let her lie down again. Concerned, he looked at Scottie, silently asking her if there was a problem.

Scottie just shook her head, dismissing his question and praying she was right.

"Okay, again, Noelle. This time push as hard as you can."

"I *ammmm*!" Noelle shrieked, screwing her eyes

shut as she bore down and pushed again with all of her might.

They went back and forth like that two more times with Noelle growing progressively weaker. She was exhausted beyond words and thinking she was unable to give anything more.

"Last time, I promise," Scottie told her. "Give this your all."

Noelle shook her head, a tear escaping out of the corner of her eye. "I…can't."

"Yes, you can," Scottie told her fiercely. "You can do this, I know you can. C'mon, Noelle, that baby wants to be here with you. *Push!*"

As she gave her pep talk, Scottie was vaguely aware of the sound of sirens in the background. Hopefully, someone had gotten a call through to the police despite the downed cell towers and power lines.

She wanted to look up to see if there was an actual ambulance in the area, but she couldn't. Noelle's baby was finally coming on the scene and she couldn't draw her eyes away, afraid that if she did, something would go wrong at the last moment.

"Just a little more," Scottie coaxed. "One more little push. You can do it, Noelle. Your baby wants to join the party."

Scottie realized that there was a tear sliding down her cheek despite her best efforts to contain her own emotions. But then, it wasn't every day she got to witness a miracle happening.

And then, after what felt like forever, a muffled cry filled the air.

With trembling hands, Scottie supported and eased the newest Cavanaugh out into the world.

They did it!

"Congratulations, Noelle. You have a beautiful son," Scottie told her, holding the small, brand-new life in her hands.

It was hard to say who cried more, Noelle, Scottie or the baby who had just entered the world. The baby was louder, though.

Chapter 9

Tamping down the emotions that were welling up and running rampant within her, Scottie looked over Noelle's head at her partner.

"I need your shirt, Cavanaugh," she told him. "We have to wrap the baby up in something and it's either your shirt or your jacket."

"Shirt it is," Bryce volunteered. It was the less costly of the two items since his jacket had set him back a bit.

He quickly shed his jacket and stripped off his shirt, holding it out to Scottie.

With the baby in one arm, she managed to wrap the infant up in Bryce's light blue shirt and then pass the newborn into Noelle's arms.

"Ten fingers, ten toes. Perfect," Scottie pronounced, smiling warmly at the woman.

Exhausted, Noelle beamed at her son. Then, looking up, her eyes swept over the two people who had come to her aid. "Thank you," she told them, emotion brimming in her voice.

"Hey, you did all the work," Scottie pointed out, raising her voice so she could be heard above the sound of the approaching siren. Within moments, the ambulance finally reached them.

Scottie backed out of the vehicle, suddenly aware of the dull ache shooting all through her body as a protest because of the position she'd had to assume to help Noelle.

Her place was immediately taken by one of the two EMTs. They had come in response to the 9-1-1 call one of the nearby motorists had been able to make.

"Looks like someone did all our work for us," the taller of the two EMTs said. "Now, let's get you and your baby to the hospital."

Stepping out of the way, Bryce waited for the attendants to get Noelle and her baby onto the gurney.

"Bryce?" Noelle's voice was reedy as she tried to get a better view so she could see him.

"Don't worry. We'll be right behind you," he told his sister-in-law as the EMTs pushed her gurney right past him.

"Somebody's got to call Duncan—and Lucy," Noelle reminded her brother-in-law as the EMTs loaded her gurney onto the ambulance.

"Consider it taken care of," Bryce promised, raising his voice so that she could hear him. The next moment, the ambulance doors were closed.

Experiencing a flood of emotion, Bryce turned toward Scottie, who was standing right next to him. Impulsively he pulled her to him in a one-armed embrace.

The next moment, still dealing with overwhelming emotion, he gave in to what he was feeling and kissed her. Hard.

Caught completely by surprise, Scottie was stunned. A cry of protest instantly rose to her lips, but died just as quickly, melting into the atmosphere as something else came to take its place. Something hot and overwhelming.

A liquid smile felt as if flooded all through her.

For a second she allowed the feeling to settle in as she sought to get her bearings. And then, coming out of her trance, she pushed Bryce back, away from her.

"What was that for?" she demanded, doing her best not to pant.

Rather than being annoyed or taking offense, Bryce was grinning ear to ear. "For being there," he answered. "C'mon, let's go before some enterprising young cop decides to give us a ticket for driving on the sidewalk."

"Don't Cavanaughs trump everyone else?" she asked, hurrying back to his vehicle with him.

"Not always," he answered. Getting into his car, he started it up.

"You've got one uncle who's the chief of detectives, another uncle who heads the day shift CSI unit and one uncle who used to be the chief of police. Who in their right mind would give a Cavanaugh a ticket?" she asked as if it was a foregone conclusion that the answer was "no one."

"You'd be surprised," he answered.

They followed the ambulance the two short miles to the Aurora hospital. As Bryce drove his car, she continued to try to reach Duncan's cell phone.

Bryce was just pulling into the hospital parking lot when she finally, on her fourth attempt, managed to get through to his brother.

"Cavanaugh."

His voice sounded strangely like Bryce's. Without announcing herself, she said, "Detective Cavanaugh, you're the proud father of a baby boy."

"Who is this?" Duncan cried.

"You probably don't remember me," she told him. She caught the side-glance Bryce gave her. "This is Alexandra Scott. We met last night at Malone's. I'm calling to tell you that your wife was just brought to Aurora General."

"I'm on my way!" Duncan cried, abruptly terminating the call.

Smiling to herself, Scottie tucked her phone away and got out of the car. "Mission accomplished," she told Bryce.

"In more ways than one," he said, leading the way into the hospital lobby.

Looking over his shoulder, he saw that Scottie wasn't directly behind him. She was hanging back.

"C'mon," he urged, beckoning her forward. "You're part of all this now."

She wasn't sure how he meant that, but she supposed this was not the time to lag behind. With a shrug, Scottie picked up her pace.

"You know," the heavyset nurse said, putting her hands on her hips as she surveyed the large group of Aurora police detectives and officers that had descended on the maternity floor, "whenever there's this large an influx of Cavanaughs, it's because one of you had been shot and you're keeping vigil."

A longtime veteran at the hospital, the head nurse shook her head as she tried her best to herd family members into the waiting room.

"I know." Andrew Cavanaugh smiled broadly at the nurse. "This is much better. Celebrating a brand-new life coming into the world," the former chief of police enthused. "Just think of all the possibilities."

The nurse shook her head. "I'm just thinking of trying to get through the next few hours, until the end of my shift." She pursed her lips as she looked at the clusters of law-enforcement agents and their spouses who had filled the general area. She raised her voice. "I suppose it'll do me no good to remind all of you that it's only two allowed at a bedside at any given time."

In response, Shamus Cavanaugh—Andrew, Brian and Sean's father and the recognized patriarch of the clan—hooked his arm through the nurse's and began to lead her down the hall, back to the nurses' station.

"Why don't I tell you about the first time I decided to get involved with law enforcement?"

The nurse made one futile attempt to resist. "Mr. Cavanaugh—"

"Anyone ever tell you that you've got really beautiful eyes, darlin'?"

Scottie, standing next to her partner, overheard his granduncle as the older Cavanaugh led the woman away. "Does that kind of thing actually work?" she asked Bryce, referring to the line the older man had just used on the nurse.

"More times than you would think," Andrew answered, joining them to stand in front of her and Bryce.

Scottie had turned to see who was talking to her. Before she knew it, she was caught up in what could only be described as a huge bear hug. For a moment she felt like her breath had been siphoned out of her lungs.

"I hear you helped Noelle deliver her baby," Andrew said, setting her down. "On behalf of the entire family, thank you," he pronounced warmly.

Surprised, Scottie found herself automatically returning the embrace, which was even more surprising. It wasn't like her. By nature, she'd stopped being a hugger a long time ago and now she'd been embraced twice in the last hour.

"How did you know?" she asked, mystified by the chief's greeting. Bryce had remained with her the entire time, so he couldn't have said anything to the man. So then how…?

"Word gets around," Andrew chuckled. "Besides, there's not much I don't know when it comes to my family," he assured her. More family members were coming into the waiting area. "You'll join us for the celebration?" It sounded like a question, but Scottie had a feeling that her answer was a foregone conclusion. Didn't anyone ever say no to any of these people?

"What celebration?" Scottie asked him cautiously.

When Andrew Cavanaugh smiled, the years vanished and he looked very much the way he had when he was an active police chief. "The one we're having as soon as Noelle and the baby come home from the hospital."

"She'll be there," Bryce told his uncle before she had a chance to say anything.

"Then I look forward to seeing you at my house," Andrew told her. The next moment he was slipping away. "Excuse me. I'd like to have a few words with the new mother," he said, taking his leave.

Floored, Scottie looked at her partner. "I'm beginning to see where you get your pushiness from," she murmured.

"We prefer to think of it as warmth," Bryce told her, amusement playing on his lips. "By the way, everyone's grateful to you."

She shrugged self-consciously. "If I hadn't been there, you would have done it."

Bryce was extremely grateful he hadn't been put to the test.

"Doesn't change the fact that you were the one who did do it," he pointed out. "You kept her calm and helped to bring her son into the world. That's a pretty big deal in our book."

Scottie took a gamble. "Big enough to get me out of attending whatever party your uncle has in mind?"

Bryce laughed. "Nice try. Almost, but not quite. You'll have fun," he promised. "What have you got to lose?"

"Time," Scottie said emphatically.

"Party won't be for a few days," he told her. "I take it that you want to get back to work?" Bryce guessed.

There was no hesitation on her part. "Yes!"

He looked around the waiting area. They had had more than their share of time with Noelle. It would leave more room for the others if they left.

"Okay, then, let's go," Bryce agreed. "Gridlock should be over with by now."

At this point, antsy to get back to the case, Scottie was willing to walk back to the police station if she had to as a last resort.

It turned out not to be necessary. The gridlock had, for the most part, cleared up, leaving a relatively clear road from the hospital to the police station.

They made excellent time, quickly reaching the precinct. Once there, Bryce was amazed that his partner dug right in and went back to work. He wondered if she was always this dedicated or if there

was something about this particular case that mo-
tivated her.

Maybe she was just trying to make points because
this was her first case in Robbery, he mused.

"What are you doing?" he asked her, leaning back
in his chair. It was close to half an hour later. She'd
been working intently since they'd come into the
squad room. He didn't think her fingers had been
still in all that time. They'd been flying over the
keyboard.

"I'm inputting all the information in these files—"
she nodded at the pile next to her elbow "—into an
Excel chart. Maybe the pattern will become clearer
to us once I do that."

"You know," Bryce told her, "you have earned a
little time off, considering that you spent the afternoon helping the chief's niece give birth."

"I had time off. It was called lunch," she reminded
him.

"That was before Noelle called." He crossed his
arms and studied her for a moment. "Do you ever
kick back?" he asked her.

"Only if I'm kicked first," she answered.

Bryce laughed, shaking his head. About to make
a comment about her stubbornness, he never got the
chance. The phone on his desk rang.

At the same time, so did hers.

Scottie raised her eyes, looking at her partner. She
could see that he was thinking the same thing she
was. There'd been another break-in.

They weren't wrong.

The break-in had taken place two blocks away from the victims they had questioned earlier this morning. It was almost as if the thieves had gone full circle and were starting on another round.

"Want to hear my theory?" Bryce asked as he drove them to the site of the latest break-in.

"Could I stop you?" Scottie quipped. When he gave her a look, she waved him on. "Go ahead."

"I think the thief or thieves took advantage of today's gridlock. He or she—or they—knew that the victim they'd planned to target next wouldn't be able to get back to the house for several hours because of the downed traffic lights."

She nodded. "Sounds logical. But gridlock works two ways. How did the thief, or thieves, get away?" she asked him.

"On foot most likely. They wouldn't risk getting stuck in this traffic."

She thought about the implication of what Bryce had just said. "That meant that they took only what they could carry on their person."

He'd seen Scottie pack the files into her messenger bag as they'd left the squad room. "Go over the list of other break-ins again," he instructed. "I think we might have found their specialty."

She didn't have to go over the lists, or ask what he thought the thieves' "specialty" was. She didn't have to hazard a guess. She knew. The thief or thieves were taking jewelry, rare coins and cash, all easily carried off in their pockets—or possibly just a small bag—without raising any suspicions.

A sinking feeling took hold of the pit of her stomach. They kept coming back to rare coins, Ethan's hobby.

"Hey, are you all right?" Bryce questioned as they pulled up in front of the latest break-in victims' house. "You look a little pale."

"Must be the lighting," she joked, dismissing his concern.

Raymond Miller was on several boards of directors and his wife, Grace, spent her time chairing charity events. Both were known to be generous to a fault and right now, both felt as if they weren't safe in the home they'd thought of as their haven.

"How could this have happened?" Miller asked. "I've got a top-of-the-line security system, a smarthouse and so many safeguards in place that I have to carry around a book to remember all the passwords."

"Anything that can be created can be hacked, sir," Bryce told him patiently.

"Apparently," Miller grumbled. "It's all insured," he told the detectives. "But still, I can't shake the feeling that I've been..." His voice trailed off.

"Violated." His wife spoke up, supplied the word.

"We understand how you feel," Scottie told the couple. "We're doing what we can to catch these thieves. We'd like to ask you a few questions so that we can come up with a profile of the people who broke into your house."

"Do you really think you can catch them?" Miller asked.

"We're damn well going to try," Bryce promised the couple.

They left with the Millers' statement and a list of what had been stolen as well as the name of their insurance company and the company that had installed their security system. Neither was familiar or matched the names of the ones used by the other victims.

Frustrated, Scottie turned down Bryce's invitation to go out after hours and raise a toast to the newest Cavanaugh. She begged off, claiming that she was exhausted down to the bone—and she was.

But that didn't keep her from swinging by her brother's apartment on her way home.

He still wasn't there.

And he still wasn't answering his phone.

Something, she knew, was very, very wrong. Ethan didn't have her dedication and serious temperament, but he wasn't a flake, either. He wouldn't just take off or disappear this way. Something was off, she knew it, but if she asked for help in locating him, his life would be placed under a microscope and closely examined. She couldn't risk that. *Especially* if he was involved with whoever was pulling off these break-ins and she was beginning to have a progressively less than good feeling about that.

She went to sleep dressed, with her cell phone

right next to her just in case she got an urgent call from Ethan in the middle of the night.

No call came.

What did come was a completely unwanted dream that replayed, in vivid terms and all sorts of startling, blazing colors, the sudden kiss she'd been pulled into without warning.

Bryce's kiss.

After she'd relived it twice, each time more intensely than the last, she bolted upright. For a second she searched the immediate area around her, expecting to find Bryce there.

All she found were the same shadows that had been there when she'd fallen asleep.

"Damn it, Cavanaugh, I've got enough to deal with. Why are you in my head?" she demanded, scrubbing her hands over her face.

There was no answer to that, other than he'd just caught her off guard, and…okay, the man really knew how to kiss, but so what? She wasn't in the market for a man who could curl her toes and raise her body temperature by ten degrees.

What am I in the market for? she silently asked herself.

"Answers," she said out loud. "I want answers. Where the hell are you, Ethan, and who the hell is pulling off these break-ins?"

She got out of bed, knowing she might as well get ready because there wasn't going to be any more sleep for her. And she definitely didn't want to have that dream again.

"If I find out that you've got a hand in it, that you let yourself be sucked into this, you're going to be really sorry, Ethan," she swore.

What she was afraid of was that she was going to be sorry, as well.

Chapter 10

"Have you tried a hot shower and warm milk?" Bryce asked his partner as he sat at his desk several mornings later.

Lost in thought, Scottie didn't hear him at first. She was only aware that Bryce had said something. Scrolling to the next page on her computer screen, she asked, "What?"

Bryce pushed the container of coffee he had brought in for her a little closer to her on her desk so that she would see it, then sat back in his chair and took the top off his own container.

"I said, have you tried a hot shower and warm milk? To help you go to sleep," he added when she looked at him quizzically. "Because, clearly, you're still not getting enough."

She dismissed his concern. "I don't need much sleep," Scottie said.

He didn't know about that. "It's obvious that you need more than you're getting."

This time she did look up at him. "Because I look awful?" she challenged.

"Because you look tired," he told her. "You've got a long way to go before you look awful."

That caught her off guard. "Is that a compliment, Cavanaugh?"

He didn't know if she'd take what he'd just said as an insult. With Scottie, it was hard to tell. "Don't get your back up," he counseled. "That was just an observation."

"I was up early, working the case," Scottie told him, which was, in its own way, a half truth. She was up, working the case because she was having trouble sleeping and that was case-related because she was worried about Ethan.

"No case is worth working yourself into the ground over," he told her. He paused to take a long sip of his extra-strong coffee. "Seriously, there are different sleep remedies you could try."

"Thanks, but I'll deal with this myself." She looked at the container in her hand. The one she'd started drinking from without thinking. With a sigh, she put it down on her desk. "And you don't have to keep bringing me coffee."

He shrugged. "It's the least I can do after what you did for Noelle."

She didn't want him making a big deal out of it,

didn't want any sort of extra attention thrown her way. "I would have done it for any woman in that condition."

"Yes, but it doesn't change the fact that you did it for Noelle." He looked at his partner for a long moment, trying to figure her out. "Why is it so hard for you to just accept thanks?"

Because accepting thanks was the first step toward getting close to someone and she didn't want to be close to anyone because that never ended well. She summed up her feelings by saying, "Because it opens up doors I don't want open."

She had to have gotten that philosophy from someone, Bryce judged. People weren't born loners. "Everyone in your family like you?"

She went back to her online search. "There *is* no one in my family." Maybe he'd stop probing now.

"Only child?" Bryce guessed. "Orphan?"

She should have known better, she thought, exasperated. "I came riding in from the ocean on an open seashell," she told him tersely. "*Now* can you please just let me concentrate on my work?"

Rather than saying yes or retreating, Bryce came around to her side of the desk and looked over her shoulder. "Okay, Venus," he said, referring to the image she'd just described of a famous painting. And then he looked at her monitor. She was tracking someone's credit card. "Who's Eva Wilkins?"

Why couldn't he just stay on his own side of the desk? "Just a name that popped up."

"When?" he asked. "I was with you when we

questioned all of the break-in victims these last few days and that name never came up in any of the conversations. Neither is it in any of the files," he pointed out and then he looked at her more closely. Scottie was hiding something. "So, who is she?"

It had taken her two days to remember the last name of the woman Ethan's neighbor had described seeing. She had credit reports belonging to the woman open on her monitor. They hadn't been easy to get and she knew that Cavanaugh knew that. He wasn't going to back off until she gave him an answer.

"Just someone who might have some decent information on the case," she told him.

Bryce turned her chair around so that she was facing him squarely. He wasn't about to continue talking to the back of her head.

"You know, part of the beauty of working together is that we *work together*," he stressed. "That means we share ideas, hunches and information with each other. Now I might not be the world's greatest detective, but I do have the ability to recall details and names associated with the case I'm currently working on. This woman's name never came up. Now who is she, Scottie?" he asked. "A witness? A possible suspect?"

Scottie's mind scrambled for something plausible to tell her partner. She didn't want to tell him that the woman had been her brother's girlfriend and had managed to get him entrenched with a gang of cyber thieves who'd used their expertise to pull off robberies. Ethan had turned out to be sharper than any of them and was soon their main asset. He'd done it because Eva had asked him to. Eva had been her brother's weakness. He hadn't been able to say no to her.

She'd thought, when she had intervened, that Eva was a thing of the past and he wasn't going to ever see her again.

Obviously she hadn't counted on the woman's determination.

"She's a hacker," Scottie grudgingly told him.

Bryce shook his head. "Never heard of her."

"That's because she's a very *good* hacker." Scottie emphasized the word.

He looked back at the monitor. So far, he didn't see any suspicious activity to indicate that this Eva Wilkins was spending large amounts of money. "So you think hackers are behind the break-ins?"

She decided to tell Cavanaugh part of what she had figured out, just not enough to turn him onto Ethan if her brother was involved.

"I think they're instrumental in at least laying down the groundwork. Think about it. Only certain things are being stolen from the houses that have been broken into. One way to hone in on who has what is to hack into insurance companies that deal in home owners insurance. People who take out extra insurance on their things—like art, jewelry, *coin collections*," she stressed, "have to list those items in their insurance policies. You hack into the insurance company's database, find out who has things worth stealing, and half your work is done."

"That's impressive," he said, referring to what she had figured out. "But how do they manage to break in when no one's home?"

She had an idea about that, as well, but for now she was keeping it to herself until she could ascertain if it was viable or not.

"I'm working on that."

"You're new to the department," Bryce said abruptly.

Where had that come from? "Yes? So?"

"So how do you know all this?" he asked, gesturing at her computer screen.

"I read a lot of mystery books," she told him dismissively, hoping that would be the end of the discussion on that subject.

"And this Eva Wilkins...how do you know about her?" he asked.

She didn't want to tell him about Ethan, so she couldn't tell him about Eva's connection to her brother. "A girl's got to have some secrets, doesn't she?" Scottie said vaguely.

He wasn't about to play that game. "Not from her partner."

"Sometimes especially from her partner," she said pointedly. Her eyes met his for a long moment before she said, "It's called giving you plausible deniability."

She was telling him she was giving him an alibi, just in case. This wasn't making any sense. "You just made that up."

Well, logic isn't working. She gave emotion a try. "Can we please stop talking and just let me follow my hunch?"

"Sure," he told her easily. "As long as I follow it with you."

Okay, this was getting annoying, she thought, frowning. "You weren't joined at the hip to your last partner," she reminded him.

"I'm trying out something new," he countered flippantly.

Under normal circumstances she might have found this a bit intriguing, or challenging, but these weren't normal circumstances. She was intent on finding the thieves and at the same time saving her brother if it came down to that. For that, she needed space, not a shadow.

"Hey," Bryce said suddenly, pointing to a line on the monitor, "it looks like this Eva person just used her credit card at a pharmacy not too far from here to buy an inhaler. Looks like our girl has asthma."

A red flag went up in her head. Her brother had asthma. She looked closely at the charge. Eva was getting the inhaler for him, not herself. That told her that, if nothing else, Ethan was with Eva.

"Yes, it does," Scottie murmured.

She sounded almost preoccupied as she agreed, Bryce noted. He was struck by her lack of enthusiasm about this piece of information. And then it hit him why. "You already knew that," he guessed.

She said no, but there was next to no conviction behind the word.

This was possibly the first lead they'd had in several days. Bryce was ready to go with it.

"I'm going to pull her photo off her DMV license and we'll show that to the pharmacy clerk, see if he recognizes her and if he has a current address on file for her."

"I can do that," she told her partner. "That way, you can follow up on any other leads."

He looked at her. Hadn't she been paying attention? "There are no other leads," he pointed out.

She seemed very anxious to get rid of him, he thought, and couldn't help wondering why.

Had she been someone else, he might have thought she was trying to take all the credit for herself, but she didn't strike him as the type. They'd only been working together a few days, but he prided himself on his ability to read people and she wasn't a glory hound like some other detectives had turned out to be.

Something else was going on here, Bryce thought. But what?

"Oh." She felt a little deflated. If there were no other leads, then he was coming with her. She couldn't very well shake him. "And you don't have anything else you want to do?"

"I'd like to sail around the world someday, but not until we solve this case," he told her. "If *you* want to sit this out for some reason…" He let his voice trail off, waiting for her to either protest or agree to be left behind.

Even if Ethan wasn't involved in this, there was

no way she wanted to sit this out. "No, I want to be in on this," she told him.

She already knew that the address on Eva's DMV license was bogus. If the pharmacy had the woman's actual address, she definitely wanted it.

"Then let's go," he said, taking the DMV photograph he had just reproduced on the printer and tucking it into his pocket.

The pharmacy clerk squinted at the photograph Bryce held up for him.

"Her hair doesn't look like that anymore," he commented. "It's all these different colors now, like a peacock, but, yeah, I've seen her. She was here yesterday, picking up a prescription for somebody."

Bryce put the photograph away. "Who?" he asked.

The clerk shook his head. "Sorry. Privacy laws," the clerk explained. "They prevent me from giving you that information."

Bryce held up his badge to drive his point home. "This is a crime investigation," he told the clerk.

The clerk obviously thought of the most prevalent crime that affected him. "You mean that prescription was a phony?"

Bryce was about to set the clerk straight but then stopped himself. If this misunderstanding made the clerk more compliant about the information he needed, namely the woman's address, so much the better.

"We're checking that out," he said vaguely.

"Just a minute," the clerk told him and then went

to his computer to pull up the screen that gave him the information he needed. "Says here that the prescription was written for E—"

Alerted, Scottie was quick to cut in before he said any more. "Why don't you print that up for us?" she requested.

"Sure." The clerk hurried off to comply.

"Looks like we're finally getting somewhere," Bryce commented.

"Hopefully," she replied.

She didn't sound all that confident, Bryce thought. What she sounded like was uneasy.

Why?

A couple of minutes later the clerk returned with the printout she'd requested. He held it out to Bryce but before he could take it, Scottie interceded and took the printout from him.

"Thank you. You've been a great help. A lot of people owe you a debt of gratitude," she told the startled-looking clerk, folding the page in two and tucking it into her messenger bag.

"Um, always glad to help the Aurora P.D.," the clerk called out after them as they left the pharmacy.

Bryce made no comment. He waited until they were both inside the car and he was once again behind the wheel. Then, instead of starting up his vehicle, he looked at Scottie.

"Why don't you want me to look at the paper?" he asked.

"It's not that I don't want you to look at it," she told him. "I'm just trying to lighten your load a little."

He wasn't buying that for a second. "We share the load," he pointed out.

Scottie knew how to twist and turn with the current and went with that. "Exactly. And going to question this woman is just me shouldering my share of the burden."

But Bryce continued to sit there. Rather than start the car, he took out the DMV photo they had showed the clerk. "You want to tell me about this woman?" he asked quietly.

She could feel her pulse accelerating. That didn't usually happen anymore because she'd gotten very good at looking someone in the eye and lying when she had to. But it wasn't something she wanted to do.

Taking a breath, Scottie tried to sound positive as she said, "I thought I already did. She's a hacker with a sealed juvenile record. I've got a feeling that she might have a hand in this."

He didn't ask her why, the way she expected him to. Instead he hit her with "How do you know her?"

Her mind scrambled as she searched for something plausible to tell him.

"Her name came up in another case," she told him vaguely. That was true. It was that juvie case she'd mentioned.

"I thought you only worked homicides before you came to my department."

"I did, but not everything is cut-and-dry." She thought of Eva's backstory, or at least the one she'd given the authorities. "Her parents were killed when she was a kid. She did what she could to get by."

Bryce nodded as he continued to listen. Some of the pieces were finally coming together. "You mean like hacking."

"Like hacking," Scottie echoed.

His eyebrows drew together as he looked at her doubtfully. "And that's your only connection to her?" he asked.

"Yes." She went on the defensive before she could think better of it. "Why are you asking me all these questions?"

Bryce blew out a breath. "I guess I'm just trying to get you to trust me."

"And you think you're going to accomplish that by interrogating me?" Scottie questioned incredulously.

That was her own damn fault, Bryce thought grudgingly. He could feel himself losing his temper and he struggled to rein it in.

"I wouldn't have to resort to that if you volunteered information."

"Look, if you wanted a chatterbox who never stopped talking and didn't have a thought in her head that she didn't immediately share with the world at large, then maybe you should ask Handel for another partner," she told him, annoyed.

Part of her was tempted to get out of the car and walk, but that was pointless.

"You do know that there's a happy medium between being a chatterbox and a monk who's taken a vow of silence, right?" Bryce asked.

Scottie sighed. They were just wasting time, going

around and around about this. She'd told him as much as she intended to.

"Look, my hunch about this woman got us here and it might help to get us closer to solving this case. Isn't that enough?"

He could see that, for now, that was all she was about to share. He obviously needed to work on her some more before she was ready to come around and trust him. And trusting him was the goal.

The fastest way, he surmised, was to get her to warm up to him and see him as more than just someone she worked with. "I guess it'll have to be. For now," he added as he started his car.

Finally! she thought. "I'm beginning to understand why your last partner opted for another line of work," she said. "You could drive a saint crazy."

"I guess it's lucky for us that neither one of us is a saint."

She stared at his profile in silence as they drove, trying to figure out just what he'd meant by that and if she should be insulted—or worried.

Chapter 11

"You're sure this is the address that girl gave the pharmacy clerk?" Bryce asked as he brought his sedan to a stop a stone's throw from the pier. Just beyond that he could see the Pacific Ocean. There was no sign of any buildings.

"Well, unless that asthma patient was part guppy, that woman gave the clerk a bogus address for him," Scottie told him, crumpling the printout she was holding.

"You think?" Bryce asked, annoyed that they'd come to another dead end. He put his hand out to Scottie. "Let me take a look at that printout the pharmacy clerk gave you."

Scottie made no move to surrender the crumpled paper. "Why? Don't you think I can read?"

Her reaction, despite the feisty nature he'd come to expect, was a bit unusual. He began to wonder if his new partner *was* hiding something. "You do realize that the more you resist letting me see that printout, the more curious it makes me?"

Aware of her mistake, Scottie did her best to try to cover it up with banter. "Well, a little bit of curiosity could be a good thing. It does make life more interesting."

Bryce continued to hold his hand out, waiting. For once he didn't look amused. "The printout, Scottie?"

Scottie suppressed a sigh. She really had no options open to her. If they were standing outside right now, she could accidentally let the breeze capture the paper and take it away. But there were no breezes in the car and she had no recourse but to give him what he wanted. Reluctantly, not sure what he could glean from the printout, she surrendered the paper.

As she did so, she told Bryce, "You really need to work on your trust issues."

"That's a little like the pot calling the kettle black, isn't it?" he pointed out. Smoothing out the paper she'd handed over, Bryce took a look at the information they had gotten from the pharmacy clerk. "'Ethan Loomis,'" he read. He glanced up at Scottie. "This has got to be her partner."

"Not necessarily," Scottie was quick to argue. "This might just be someone Eva was running an errand for. You know, this could represent her one good deed." When Bryce looked at her, the expression on his face telling her that he clearly was not buying it, she shrugged. "I mean, it could be."

He wondered if she believed what she was saying. "What are the odds of that?" he asked.

Scottie was forced to shrug her shoulders. She knew she was on weak ground. "I don't know. I'm just saying that nothing is set in stone. The guy could be her brother."

"Different last names," he pointed out.

"It happens," she responded.

"True," he agreed, "but my gut says that this 'Ethan Loomis' is involved in this somehow."

That made two of them, Scottie thought, but she did her best to try to talk her partner out of it.

"And your gut is always right?" she asked him skeptically.

"Pretty much," Bryce answered. "Definitely enough to see if we can find any background information on this Ethan Loomis."

Until she knew exactly what was going on, she needed to get ahead of this, to play interference if she could.

"Why don't I see what I can find?" Scottie offered, doing her very best to sound helpful and eager.

Bryce started his car again, making a three-point turn to go back the way they had come. Since this had turned out to be a dead end, he decided to drive back to the precinct.

"Okay, you do that." He made a sharp right at the corner then spared her a glance. "Oh, by the way, it's at one tomorrow."

Trying to plan her next move and how to divert Bryce away from her brother, his last words confused her. "What's at one tomorrow?"

He'd had a feeling that she'd "conveniently" forget. "The party that Uncle Andrew is throwing to celebrate the birth of the newest Cavanaugh."

Oh, damn. That. The whole idea of a party had slipped her mind. The last thing she wanted to do was to attend a gathering and be surrounded with celebrating Cavanaughs, not in her present frame of mind.

"Well, I hope you have a really nice time," she told him.

He'd expected this. "I don't think you get it, 'partner.' Celebrating the birth of the newest Cavanaugh doesn't just involve the family, in this case it also involves the person who helped bring that life into the world."

"You were there, too," she reminded him, hoping this little bit of logic would be sufficient in running interference in this case.

Bryce was not about to be dissuaded. He grinned at her, thinking that she was rather cute, trying to talk her way out of this. She had to know by now that she was coming to the party even if he had to hog-tie her and carry her there.

"You were there more," he said pointedly. He was still smiling at her, but it was clear he was not about to give in.

"Tomorrow at one?" Scottie asked as if it was the first time she'd heard it.

"Uh-huh." He had a feeling she was up to something and he braced for it.

"Sorry, I can't make it," she told him in all seriousness. "I have plans."

"From the intel I've gathered about you, you *never* have plans."

She wasn't accustomed to people poking around in her life. "What do you mean 'from the intel' you've gathered? Have you been asking around about me?" Scottie asked. She could feel her back going up.

Bryce proceeded with caution, tempering his answer. He had no desire to make her angry. His goal was to make her agreeable—or as agreeable as she was capable of being.

"I have family working in Homicide," he reminded her casually. "They had good things to say about you," Bryce began. "But they all agree you're not a mingler."

"'All'?" she echoed. It sounded like he had taken a massive interdepartmental survey. "Just how many people did you talk to?"

She was still on the defensive. Bryce walked his statement back. "Just a few."

Scottie did her best to restore peace between them and still put an end to the discussion. Why couldn't he—and his family—leave her alone? She was aware that he just meant well, but that wasn't the end result.

"Well, then you know I don't join in these kinds of things. Parties, I mean," she clarified.

Bryce nodded. She'd just made his point for him. "Which is how I know you don't have plans."

She pressed her lips together. He got her. "I kind of walked into that one, didn't I?"

"That you did," he told her with a wide, sexy smile that she was finding she was having a harder and harder time resisting. "So, when should I pick you up?"

Oh, hell, the last thing she wanted was for him to escort her to the party.

"You shouldn't," she told him. "I'm perfectly capable of driving myself over if you give me the address."

"Driving isn't the problem," he told her simply. "Parking is."

"Excuse me?"

"This is going to be a full-scale, pull-out-all-the-stops kind of party," he told her. His uncle, he knew, had already started cooking in preparation for tomorrow. The whole family was coming, as well as a great many friends. "Most, if not all, of the family will be there," he told her. "Which means that if you hope to find a parking spot in the same zip code as Andrew's house, carpooling with me is the only answer."

Scottie looked at him. "I see through that, you know," she told him. "You just don't trust me to go."

He laughed. "Well, there's that, too. But parking really will be a colossal bear," he told her honestly. "Uncle Andrew encourages everyone to at least double up if possible." Her resistance brought up a host of questions in his mind. "C'mon, Scottie, what are you afraid of?"

That made her back go up immediately. "I'm not afraid of anything," she insisted.

He pretended to believe her and dropped the subject. "Good, then I'll be by to pick you up at one."

She frowned, knowing it would do her no good to argue about it. She'd already learned that he wasn't the type to give up. Ever.

"Fine. I'll be ready at one. Now is it okay with you if I try to find some information on this Ethan Loomis?" she asked sarcastically.

"I'm counting on it," Bryce answered as they pulled up into the police department's parking lot.

Her plan was to compile just enough information on her brother to give Bryce *something*, but not enough to send him in the right direction to look for Ethan.

But she discovered that she didn't need to worry. Undertaking a search for Ethan, she found that there was nothing to give Bryce, substantial or otherwise. Ethan had somehow managed to eliminate any and all digital footprints that lead to him. As far as the internet was concerned, her brother didn't exist.

That made her worry even more.

Scottie went from one site to another with the same results. "There's nothing here," she said out loud, stunned.

Busy pursuing another avenue of investigation, Bryce looked up from his computer. "What did you say?"

Frustration had her wanting to pound her fist on

the keyboard. Restraining herself wasn't easy. "I said there's nothing here. On Ethan," she clarified.

"You sound surprised," he noted. "It's probably an alias. And this Ethan, or whatever his name really is, wasn't smart enough to create a corresponding identity for his alias," he surmised.

Scottie started to say something then decided it was best just to agree with Bryce. If he thought Ethan's name was an alias, at least he wouldn't be looking into her brother.

The problem was, right now, neither could she, and that drove her absolutely crazy. Ethan must have found a way to erase all traces of himself. He wouldn't have done that without a reason.

Just how deep are you in this? she silently demanded of her brother.

"Probably," Scottie agreed out loud, struggling not to let Bryce see just how upset all of this made her.

She didn't have much time, Scottie thought, glancing at her watch the next day. It was almost twelve. Cavanaugh had said he'd be by at one to pick her up and she intended to be long gone by then. If he asked her about it come Monday morning, she was just going to tell him she'd found a possible lead to pursue—one that wound up leading nowhere—and had forgotten all about the party she'd promised to attend.

Hurrying, Scottie didn't even bother checking her makeup as she grabbed her purse and headed for the front door. Yanking it open, she stifled a scream as she stumbled backward.

Her escape route was blocked by all six foot two of her partner.

Clearing her throat and trying to regain her composure, Scottie demanded indignantly, "What are you doing here?"

He looked at her as if she'd had a complete loss of memory. "Picking you up for the party, remember?"

"You weren't supposed to be here until one," she retorted.

His smile was guileless and despite the fact that she was annoyed with him, she had to admit it was almost lethally sexy. She blamed her annoying reaction on that unexpected kiss that had happened right after the ambulance had taken Noelle and her baby to the hospital. Over and over again, she'd tried to tell herself it was "just one of those things" but it had turned out to be one of those things that insisted on lingering. Indefinitely.

"Sometimes I'm early," Bryce told her. "This is one of those times. Good thing, too, because you looked like I just caught you on your way out. You weren't thinking of pulling a vanishing act now, were you?"

The question sounded innocent enough but the expression on Bryce's face told her he already knew the answer.

She gave squirming out of the invitation one final try. "This is a family gathering you're having. I'm going to be out of place there."

If that was the best argument she had to offer, Bryce thought, then he'd already won. "As my uncle Andrew likes to say, there are a lot of definitions of the word *family*. Blood is not the only criteria. You, for instance, belong to the family of law-enforcement agents."

"So did J. Edgar Hoover," she countered. "I don't think you would have wanted him attending your family gathering."

"Can't really say," he told her. "But I do know that Noelle asked me if you were coming."

"Really?"

He was just saying that, Scottie thought. The man was as stubborn as they came. If she'd acted indifferent to the invitation in the first place, she had a feeling he wouldn't be pushing nearly this hard. She should have realized it was the challenge that engaged him.

"Really," Bryce assured her. "So did Duncan." His eyes held hers as he told her, "So did Uncle Andrew."

Okay, he was making all this up. "They wouldn't even know if I didn't show up," she insisted. "Not with all those people attending."

"They'd know," he told her with certainty. Putting his hand to the small of her back, Bryce gently but forcefully ushered her out the door. "C'mon, Scottie. You've got nothing to lose and maybe, just maybe, something to gain," he coaxed. Getting her outside, he pulled the front door shut behind him. "I do know that you could use the break."

She reached into her purse for her keys, but even as she did so, she challenged, "And if I said no?"

His eyes met hers. Just for a moment, held her prisoner. "Don't," he told her quietly.

She sighed and locked her door. Dropping her keys into her purse, she followed him to his car, which was parked in her driveway. She was still trying to bargain. "Can I set a time limit?"

"Sure." Bryce had no desire to come off too unreasonable.

"Half an hour," she said as she got into the vehicle.

Getting in himself, Bryce gave her a look that told her what he thought of her suggestion.

"A reasonable time limit," he elaborated. "Like two hours."

One hundred and twenty minutes. That was longer than she was happy about, but still, she supposed she could live with it. "And if after two hours, I want to leave, you'll let me?"

He nodded. "I'll bring you right back to your front door without any complaint," he promised. "Do we have a deal?"

She had no choice but to agree. But he was a man of his word so she was going to trust that he would let her leave when she wanted to.

"We have a deal," she told him reluctantly.

"Good." He turned the ignition on. "I knew you'd come around."

He made it sound like this was a good thing. She saw it as a huge inconvenience. She was only going along for the sake of peace. "You don't have to look so happy about it."

"I could scowl if you want," Bryce offered, then did just that, giving her a preview.

Scottie waved his words away and turned her face toward the side window, watching the scenery going by quickly. If it wasn't for the fact that she was worried about Ethan, she supposed there was a chance she could enjoy herself, at least a little. But she *was* worried and that made all the difference in the world.

"What I want," she told him, "is to understand why it's so important for me to attend."

"I think we've already had this conversation," he reminded her patiently. For the sake of harmony, he went over it again. "Because if you hadn't been there, things might have gone very wrong. The family just wants to show their gratitude and this is the best way they know how." Bryce paused for a moment then asked, "Want my advice?"

She shifted and faced forward. "I don't think I have a choice. Go ahead."

"Just sit back and enjoy this afternoon. Who knows? It might even be good for you."

She slanted a look at him. "I wouldn't count on it. But, okay, I'll give this a shot. For two hours," she confirmed, her tone underscoring the time limit.

It didn't take long to reach their destination. She was surprised at how close she lived to the former chief. She was even more surprised when they finally arrived in the vicinity of Andrew Cavanaugh's house, that there were more cars parked in and around the area than on the lot of a used-car dealership.

Her eyes widened as she took in the sight. "You weren't kidding about all the cars parked around here."

"No, I wasn't," he agreed good-naturedly.

She gave up counting the number of cars. Obviously this party was going to be huge. "Just proves my point. I wouldn't be missed if I wasn't here."

"You'd be missed," Bryce assured her, scanning the area for an open spot. "Haven't you figured it out yet? You're not just a cog in the machinery. You're part of the team, Scottie. Time to really get to know them away from the crime scenes and the autopsy reports and all the rest of it."

All she said in response was, "You said two hours, right?"

He decided to stop trying to sell her on the idea. Attending the party would do it for him. "Two hours," he repeated.

"That is, if we even find parking," Scottie noted, looking at the daisy chain of automobiles.

"This isn't as bad as it can get," Bryce told her.

She couldn't picture it getting any worse. "Maybe you people should rent a bus, like they do for school field trips." She was only half kidding.

"There's an idea," Bryce commented. "You might want to pass that along to Uncle Andrew."

Right, like he would take any advice from an outsider, she thought. And then she sat straighter.

"There's a space right there," she told him, spotting one near the end of the next block.

"I see it." He headed straight for it, managing to effortlessly pull in between two cars. She didn't realize she was holding her breath until he straightened out his wheels. The man had hidden talents, she thought in grudging admiration. "We make a good team," he commented. Turning off the ignition, he said, "I want you to promise me something."

Scottie braced herself. "What?"

He got out of the car and came around to her side, prepared to help her out. She ignored the hand he offered. "That for the next two hours, you are going to relax and enjoy yourself."

She was just focused on the finish line. "And then we'll leave?"

"And then we'll leave," he told her.

He'd said it far too cheerfully. She didn't believe him, but pretended that she did. For now, as she followed him to the front door, what else could she do?

Chapter 12

"Your two hours starts now," Scottie said just as her partner rang the doorbell.

"I'll synchronize my watch," he deadpanned. A moment later the front door opened.

The former chief of police, Andrew Cavanaugh, looking decidedly younger than his age despite the mane of silver-gray hair, stood in the doorway. There was a warm smile on his unlined face as he looked from Bryce to her.

"I see you got her to come," Andrew said with approval. "I knew you would." He took Scottie's hand in both of his, gently coaxing her across the threshold and into the house itself. "Come in, come in. I'm sure you know at least a few of the people here. If not, Bryce can serve as your guide. Get her something cool to drink, Bryce. You know where everything is," he instructed, still holding Scottie's hand sandwiched between his own.

"Noelle, Duncan and the baby are on the patio. They'll be really glad to see you," Andrew went on to tell her. A pulsing buzzer went off and he looked over his shoulder toward the kitchen, releasing her hand as he did so. "Sounds like part of the main course is done, so if you'll excuse me." Inclining his head, Andrew retreated, making his way to the kitchen.

"Well, you heard the man. Let's get you watered and circulated," Bryce told her with a laugh. He slipped his arm around her shoulders as if they had been friends and comrades-in-arms for years rather than just for a short while.

Drawing her toward the back of the sprawling, spacious house, weaving in between members of his family, Bryce leaned in and whispered into her ear. "This'll all be painless, I promise."

Right now, she wasn't thinking about meeting new people. She was focusing on trying her best not to react to the way her partner's warm breath had zipped along not just her ear, but her cheek and her neck, as well, stirring her the way she definitely didn't want to be stirred.

"You don't have to patronize me," Scottie whispered back between gritted teeth.

"That wasn't patronizing," he told her in all innocence, still moving toward the patio. "That was just trying to calm you down."

She was about to tell him she didn't need that, either, but she never got the chance because, stepping out onto the patio, she suddenly found herself being swallowed up in a huge, enthusiastic hug.

"Thank you!" Duncan cried, all but lifting her off the floor. "Thank you for being there for Noelle and for bringing Scottie into the world."

"'Scottie'?" Scottie repeated, confused and trying desperately to get at least some of her bearings and her dignity back.

"Duncan, let her go before you break something," Noelle ordered, looking incredibly well for a woman who had just given birth a few days ago. As her husband released Scottie, she explained, "We're naming the baby after you."

Scottie looked from Duncan, to Noelle, to the baby in the layette situated right beside Noelle's patio chair.

"I don't know what to say," she finally managed to get out, then added, "Are you sure you want to do that?"

"Absolutely," Noelle told her without any hesitation. She linked her hand with Duncan's. "It's our small way of saying thank you."

"I was there, too," Bryce pointed out, pretending to feel slighted.

"Sorry, bro." Duncan put his hand on his brother's shoulder. "But 'Scottie Bryce' just doesn't have a good ring to it."

"Cav—Bryce has a point," Scottie said, forcing herself to use her partner's first name as she backed him up. She just wasn't used to being singled out like this and it made her feel somewhat awkward. "He was there and he *is* your brother."

"But you're family now, too," Brian Cavanaugh told her, coming up behind her to join in the discussion. Sharp green eyes looked at her and Scottie could have sworn the man was reading her mind. "No point in fighting it," he advised. "Family is defined by actions, not just by blood."

"You heard the chief," Bryce told her, putting a tall, frosted glass of lemonade into her hand. "Don't argue," he warned, his intense look underscoring his point. "You're family."

For some reason she suddenly felt a lump forming in her throat. Because she didn't trust herself to say anything coherent, Scottie stalled for time and deliberately took a long sip of the lemonade Bryce had just brought her.

All of her life, she had more or less felt as if she was on her own, struggling to survive. Granted, she'd had a mother, but Joanne Scott had been an incredibly weak woman with an addictive personality who would disappear for days, sometimes weeks on end. From a very young age, Scottie had felt like it was up to her to take care of her mother as well as her little half brother.

Ethan was her only family and she was his after their mother had overdosed. But she would have been lying if she had said there hadn't been times when she would lie in bed, fantasizing about what it would be like not to have everything on her shoulders. Fantasizing about having a loving family, a family like some of the ones she'd occasionally see on TV in half-hour comedies where rules were strategically bent but everything was always resolved within thirty minutes—not counting commercials—and most important of all, everyone within that family knew that they were loved and protected.

She had never felt that way for even a few minutes of her life, much less a day.

Noticing the expression on her face, the first opportunity he had, Bryce ushered her away from Duncan and his family, steering her toward one of the buffet tables in the crowded backyard.

"Want something to eat?" he asked, indicating the table nearest them as well as a couple of others, each just a few feet away. "Uncle Andrew always makes sure there's more than enough different dishes to choose from," he told her. Then, lowering his voice, he looked at her and quietly asked, "You okay?"

She didn't have to think about becoming defensive. That had become her go-to mode and it took over now. "Sure. Why wouldn't I be?"

"No reason." He kept his voice light. Nothing would be simple with this new partner of his, Bryce concluded. Still, he had a feeling that, in the end, if he stuck it out, it would be well worth it. Because there was something about Alexandra Scott that was different as well as compelling. Under that steely exterior, she was vulnerable and he intended to be there for her.

"I just thought I saw something in your eyes back

there. My mistake," he told her, willingly breezing right along to spare her having to explain anything.

Scottie paused for a moment, appearing to deliberate between a plate of fried veal cutlets and a bowl of shrimp scampi. What she was really doing was trying to decide whether or not to say anything to Bryce or just to let things go.

Although she couldn't have explained why, she decided to open up a tiny bit. Scottie spared her partner a look. "You know, you're more intuitive than I gave you credit for."

Bryce grinned. "That's me. Hard shell on the outside, soft and fluffy on the inside."

She laughed then. "You just described a piece of candy."

He winked at her and she felt her stomach do a tiny flip. "I can be sweet, too," he told her.

Scottie tried to shut down and found that she wasn't completely successful. For better or worse, Bryce had managed to bore a little hole through what she'd always thought was the impregnable wall she kept around herself.

"I'll take your word for it," she answered.

"Try the veal," a bright-eyed blonde recommended. "It's to die for." Shifting her plate over to her left hand, she extended her right hand to Scottie. "Hi, I'm Moira, one of Bryce's long-suffering sisters. We met the other night at Malone's. I'm also one of two Moiras here today." She pointed in the general direction of the house. "The other is Moira McCormick, the actress, who also happens to be one of Andrew's daughters-in-law. She's married to Shaw," Moira confided. About to say more, she abruptly stopped, a wide smile on her face. "Is your head swimming yet?" she asked Scottie knowingly.

"Actually, yes," Scottie admitted. Another first, she realized, because she didn't ordinarily admit to any shortcomings. "I feel like I should be taking notes."

"Well, I suppose you can if you want to," Moira said glibly, "but you'll get the hang of this eventually, especially if you keep coming to Uncle Andrew's get-togethers, which Bryce probably told you take place a lot."

Having mentioned Bryce, Moira's attention was drawn to her brother again. "Oh, and if this one gives you any trouble," she told Scottie, nodding at her brother, "just come find me. I'll put him in his place. I always did when we were growing up," she added proudly before she took her full plate and melted back into the milling crowd.

"She didn't," Bryce told Scottie once his sister had left. "But because it seems to mean so much to her, I let her think she did. Takes so little to make some people happy," he observed wryly. And then he glanced at Scottie. "How about you?"

Her mind was getting whiplash, Scottie thought, trying to keep up to the switching topics.

"How about me what?" she asked, having no idea what her partner was referring to.

"What does it take to make you happy?" he asked simply.

Scottie fell back on generic answers. "Peace and quiet. A solved case."

"That's it?" he questioned. "Nothing more?" He was confident there had to be even if she wasn't willing to admit it.

"I'll let you know when I figure it out," she told him.

She picked up her plate. The food looked good and she was hungry, Scottie realized. She looked around for somewhere to sit.

"Hey, you two, come join us," Brennen called out to his younger brother, waving him and Scottie over to one of the small tables set up throughout the backyard. Brennen was seated at the table with Tiana, his wife, a lively woman he had met while on the job. At the time, he'd been undercover and she had pretended to be someone else, too, determined to find her missing sister.

Glancing at Bryce, Scottie expected her partner to usher her over to the table. He surprised her by giving her a choice in the matter.

"We don't have to join them if you don't want to. I can find us a place to sit by ourselves if you feel like you need a break," he told her.

She thought the whole point of coming here was for her to mingle with different members of his extended family. "Why, are they obnoxious?"

He wasn't sure if she was being serious or not. He still wasn't able to read her a hundred percent of the time, but he was working on it.

"No, but sitting with them isn't going to give you

that peace and quiet you just mentioned you wanted," he answered.

Because he was giving her a choice, Scottie began to feel better about being there. And, if she was being completely honest, the people she was meeting were far more genuinely welcoming than she'd actually expected them to be.

Scottie smiled and shrugged. "I guess I can always get that later."

And with that, she continued to make her way over to his brother's table.

"You, Alexandra Scott, are a hard woman to read," Bryce whispered to her just before they reached Brennen's table.

His comment widened her smile. "And that's the way I like it," she answered just before she joined his older brother and sister-in-law.

The remainder of the afternoon continued on that path, with Scottie meeting one member of Bryce's family after another until she felt as if she'd met at least half the precinct, not to mention the people who had married them. Liberally sprinkled into this group were the children who were the offspring of all these Cavanaughs who had first and foremost all sworn to protect and to serve.

Before she had ever walked in the front door, Scottie had made the point that she was only going to stay at the party for two hours, but when those two hours had come and then gone, she had decided to stay a little longer.

And then a little longer than that.

Before she noticed, the sun had gone down, allowing the moon to come in and take its place. And still she remained.

It surprised Scottie that she was having such a good time. A genuinely good time. Rather than being on her guard, feeling tense and thinking she was being watched, she found that, little by little, she somehow had become relaxed.

This wasn't a pseudo dynasty that looked down on everyone else the way she'd been led to believe the Cavanaughs were wont to do. The Cavanaughs she had met—and Bryce had gone out of his way to introduce her to practically everyone—were really nice, warm people who went out of their way to make an outsider feel comfortable. They talked to her not because they were being polite but because they wanted to.

She couldn't remember ever feeling this at ease at a party before. Bryce had been right. This was good for her. It showed her how life could be with just a little effort. She was more determined than ever to find Ethan and to shut down whatever operation he had gotten himself involved in.

"Penny for your thoughts," Bryce said, bringing her another piece of the cake later that evening.

"If I have this, I'm liable to explode. I've eaten far too much. Everything tasted wonderful," she told him, catching Andrew's eye from across the room. "And as for that penny, Cavanaugh," she said, looking at her partner, "it's going to cost you a lot more than that to find out what I'm thinking."

Rather than laugh or say something cryptic, Bryce regarded her for a long moment. "Might be worth it."

Her eyes met his and she stifled another shiver racing up and down her spine. "It's not what you're thinking."

"You have no idea what I'm thinking," Bryce told her quietly. "And to be honest, right now, I'm kind of glad you're not a mind reader."

She cleared her throat, trying very hard to shake off the far more serious mood insisting on coming over her. "Why? Are you having impure thoughts, Cavanaugh?" she asked. It was meant to be a joke to lighten the momentarily more serious mood that seemed to be pulsating between them.

Bryce completely floored her when he said, "I plead the fifth."

She looked at him then, suddenly feeling an onrush of heat envelop her even though she was doing her best to block that very reaction because it wasn't something she should be feeling about her partner. Her main concern—her *only* concern—was to find Ethan and pry him out of the clutches of whoever it was that was making him pull off these break-ins. That left no time for having any sort of strong, physical reactions to her partner, much less building on them.

She couldn't blame it on anything she'd had to drink because all she'd had the entire duration of the party were a few glasses of lemonade as well as soda. Whatever she was experiencing was all on her.

She needed to get a grip, Scottie told herself. To stop unconsciously wishing things were different and just deal with what was.

Most of all, she had to keep her guard up and stop drifting off, wondering what if…? There was no room for that in her life right now.

"Ready to go?" Bryce asked her.

Scottie blinked. She suddenly realized she hadn't noticed that the gathering had long since begun to thin out.

"I think those two hours you gave me are up," Bryce added, tongue in cheek.

She took a breath. Time had just seemed to whiz by. And she had really enjoyed herself. It was nice to have had this little island of time when she was just being herself. Not a detective, not someone who had to be responsible for someone else. Just herself.

She found herself being grateful to Bryce, fully aware that if she admitted any of this to Bryce, he would be just impossible to live with.

Instead she just nodded her head and said, "I guess they are."

"We can make an official exit," he told her, "or we can just slip out. Your choice."

He was giving her another choice. She'd always preferred slipping out, but it seemed rude this time. His family had all been too nice to her for her to pull a disappearing act.

"Official," she told him.

She was surprised his approving expression pleased her the way it did. "You're coming along, Detective Scott. You're really coming along."

By the time they had finally reached the front door, Scottie felt as if she had said goodbye to several generations of Cavanaughs—but not before promising to see each and every one of them "real soon." More astonishing than that, she found that they meant it.

And most astonishing of all, so did she.

Chapter 13

"So, admit it," Bryce said to her as they walked back to his car. "It wasn't as bad as you thought it was going to be."

It seemed to Scottie that her partner was almost going out of his way to be nice to her. He could have easily rubbed her nose in it, maybe even showed her a video or photos that he could have taken on his cell phone to prove she had enjoyed herself. Instead he had phrased his statement in almost neutral terms.

The man made it really difficult for her to continue to keep him at arm's length.

"Well, since you put it that way," Scottie answered. "No, today was not as bad as I thought it was going to be."

Stopping at his car, Bryce watched her, obviously waiting for her to rephrase her statement.

For thirty seconds a kind of staring contest ensued and then Scottie surrendered. "Okay, it was good. I had a good time." She raised her chin a little bit as she asked, "Satisfied?"

He wondered if she knew just how tempting a pose she had struck. It took some effort for him not to just follow through and kiss her.

"Yes," he answered, "but I was kind of hoping that you were, too."

"They're nice people," she admitted, getting into Bryce's sedan. Then she said something he hadn't expected. "I'm glad you have them in your life."

Rounding the hood, he got in on the driver's side. "I don't exactly have them under lock and key," he pointed out, buckling up. When she looked at him blankly, he added, "I'll share."

Starting up the car, he carefully pulled away from the curb. "Must be rough," he surmised, "not having any family."

Scottie pulled back a little. That was a topic she really didn't want to talk about. "You get used to it," she said with finality.

Bryce was quiet for a moment, reflecting on what she'd just said, then told her, "Personally, I think it would be kind of rough for me. It's not like I sit around, having long heart-to-hearts with my brothers and sisters, but I have to admit that it's still a good feeling to know they're there, in the background somewhere, if I ever need someone in my corner."

He glanced at her almost-rigid profile. "You're even stronger than I thought."

"You thought I was *strong*?" she questioned incredulously. If asked, she would have said that her partner didn't think about her at all.

Bryce laughed at the surprise in her voice. "You come on like a ninja warrior, so, yes, I thought you were strong." He paused for a moment then decided to push forward. "I also think that you have something on your mind."

A wariness crept into her voice. "I already told you, solving the case."

"Yeah, I know." That was what she'd said, but he wasn't buying it. "But it's more than that. Something's eating at you."

Scottie made a face. "Not unless you have fleas in your car," she quipped.

He was determined to get her to trust him enough to open up. Something was keeping her up at night and he had a feeling it had to do with the serial break-ins, although he still couldn't put his finger on what.

"I'm serious, Scottie." He infused concern into his voice. "Listen, you know if something's bothering you, you can talk to me about it."

She really wished he'd drop this. She wasn't sure just how much longer she could put him off and the last thing she wanted was for him to know that she suspected her brother was involved in the break-ins.

"So now you're a counselor?" she asked.

Rather than take offense or act like she was mocking him, Bryce took another route.

"Counselor, sounding board, occasional punching bag," Bryce added whimsically. "At one time or another, partners have to be all things to each other. The bottom line is," he told her forcefully, "that if something's bothering you, you can come to me and we'll talk it out. We'll find a solution. Together."

"'If something's bothering me,'" Scottie repeated. "You mean other than a partner who won't stop pushing?" she asked.

"If I hadn't pushed," he countered, "you would have never had a good time tonight."

Despite the topic she was trying so hard to get him to change, a whimsical smile played on her lips. "Point taken—*this time*," she amended.

Bryce gave it one more try as he pulled into her residential development. "No judgment, by the way."

Since they'd dropped the topic several minutes ago, his assertion caught her off guard. "What?"

"Whatever's bothering you," he said by way of preface. "I won't be judgmental when you tell me."

"You won't have to be because there's nothing to be judgmental about. Or to tell," she added for good measure. "I'm fine."

No, she wasn't, he thought. If she was fine, she wouldn't turn up in the office every morning looking like a zombie. A very pretty zombie, but still a zombie. "And you can't sleep because…?"

"I can't sleep," she answered with a note of final-

ity. Because he didn't look satisfied, she added for good measure, "Walk through your local pharmacy sometime. Sleeping aids are a big, thriving business. *Lots* of people can't sleep," she told him. "I just happen to be one of them."

He didn't believe her. But he couldn't exactly torture the answer out of her, either, so, for now, Bryce forced himself to let it go, promising himself to revisit the subject at a later date if she continued to look as if she had spent the night on a bed of nails.

Opening his door, he got out on his side at the same time that Scottie got out on hers.

She looked at him, startled. She had assumed he'd just remain in the car and then pull away after she got out. "Where are you going?"

Gesturing toward her house, he said, "I'm walking you to your door."

Her door was only about fifteen feet away. "Did I invite you in?" she asked, trying to remember if perhaps she had during the course of the evening and just forgotten about it.

He took a few steps in front of her, waiting for Scottie to follow suit. "No, it's just something the cop in me feels I should do."

"In case it slipped your mind, I'm a cop, too."

"Yes, you are," he readily agreed. "And right now," he continued as she began walking again, "you're a very sexy-looking cop so I'd feel better if I brought you to your door instead of having you just jump out of my car as I drove by your house."

She had stopped processing what he was saying

half a sentence ago, her attention snared by one of the words he'd used.

"You think I'm sexy?" she asked, stunned.

"Yes. I can make that observation and still be your partner," he told her matter-of-factly. "Now get your sexy self into the house."

He stood to the side as she took out her key and unlocked her door.

Turning to face him, Scottie surprised herself by asking, "*Do* you want to come in?"

He watched moonbeams getting caught in her hair, felt his hold on self-control slipping a little.

"Yes, I do," he answered honestly. That same honesty had him saying, "But right now, I don't think that would be a good idea." About to turn away, he paused, finding himself stuck on a minor point. "Knowing what you know about break-ins, why don't you have a security system?" he asked.

The question seemed almost innocuous, considering what she was bracing herself for. "There's no point to having one. If someone is *really* determined to get in, they'll find a way to override the system."

Did she believe that was always possible? Or was she more familiar with the problem than he'd thought? "Really?"

Scottie nodded.

It gave him something to think about—other than dwelling on the fact that he was an idiot for walking away after she had actually invited him in. But that route was fraught with complications and, right now, she didn't look like a woman who needed any more.

Truthfully, neither did he.

"Try to get some sleep," Bryce told her as he made his way back to his car.

"Easy for you to say," Scottie murmured under her breath as she watched her partner walk away.

There were a number of things to keep her up, not the least of which was that she was getting progressively more attracted to her partner—and she shouldn't be.

It seemed to Scottie that she had finally, *finally* managed to drift off to sleep after restlessly tossing and turning for the first three hours. Breaking into her dreamless sleep was the sound of someone ringing her doorbell.

At first she thought the sound was just part of her dream. But then her brain kicked in, alerting her that what she was hearing wasn't part of a dream—and it wasn't a drill. This was the real thing.

Someone was on her doorstep.

The next moment Scottie was completely wide awake, thinking that maybe Ethan was on the other side of her door, needing to talk to her.

She was up and out of her bedroom, flying down the stairs in a matter of seconds.

Only her intense police training kept her from throwing open the front door the second she reached it. Instead, Scottie forced herself to look through the peephole.

Her heart stopped racing then.

It wasn't her brother.

Unlocking the door, she opened it, but only partially. "Forget something?" she asked Bryce.

"Yes, you."

For the barest of seconds, his eyes swept over her, appreciatively admiring what he was looking at. Scottie, barefoot with her hair tousled, had on an oversize football jersey and, from all indication, nothing else underneath. He tamped down his imagination before it could take off on him.

Clearing his throat, Bryce asked, "How long will it take you to get dressed?"

What time was it? She looked at her watch. It was a little after four in the morning. "Are you taking me back to the ball, Fairy Godmother?" she quipped.

"No, I'm taking you to a crime scene," he told her crisply. He saw that got her attention instantly. "Apparently there's been another break-in—and this time the home owners came back unexpectedly and walked in on the thieves."

She had already started to go back upstairs to get dressed but she froze when Bryce said the home owners had surprised the thieves.

She had a bad feeling about this.

Turning around to look at Bryce, she asked, "Was anyone hurt?"

"The home owner, Jacob Williams, had a gun," he told her. "Williams said he thought he winged one of the thieves. We've got the CSI unit over there right now, going over everything to see if they can find any trace of blood."

Snapping out of her trance, trying to reassure herself that it wasn't her brother who had gotten shot, Scottie ran up the rest of the stairs two at a time.

"Give me five minutes," she called down.

"Five minutes?" Bryce echoed skeptically. "Okay, sure, but no woman in the history of the world has ever been ready in five minutes. It's physically impossible to get dressed that fast and be ready to leave in under twenty-five—" The last word dribbled out of his mouth as he looked at her. "You're back. And dressed." Had it even taken her five minutes?

"Let's go," Scottie ordered, hurrying past him as she went to the front door.

He could only stare in amazement at how fast she had put on her jeans and pullover. "How did you manage to do that?" he asked.

She supposed she could understand his surprise. Most women—hell, most people—needed more time than she'd taken.

Taking pity on him, she explained. "Growing up, I had a mother who got punchy when she was high—and by punchy, I mean she *punched*. Getting dressed and getting out of the apartment really fast was just something I picked up while trying to survive. Damn," she muttered.

For once he understood. She was annoyed with herself, not him.

"You're ticked off because you're sharing again, aren't you?" he asked with a dry laugh. "I have that effect on people. Don't worry," he told her, "I won't tell anyone."

She turned to look at him as she put her house

key into her bag, but he wasn't grinning. He looked perfectly serious as he made her what amounted to a promise.

"My upbringing isn't exactly something I'm proud of," she told him.

"You should be," he told her as they got into his car. "You survived it and turned out pretty damn well. Somebody else might not have."

"Yeah," she murmured dismissively, fastening her seat belt.

Scottie deliberately steered the conversation away from herself. "What do we know so far?" she asked, wanting to get as many details about this latest break-in as possible.

"Just that the couple was going away for an extended weekend but the wife suddenly felt sick so they turned around and came back home again. They obviously weren't expected. According to the officer taking their statement, everything outside looked just the way it had when they'd left it. There were no signs of a forced break-in, no strange vehicle parked in the street. According to Williams, there was even a flyer still hanging undisturbed on his doorknob."

Mention of a flyer instantly grabbed her attention and had her completely alert. She'd forgotten about that detail. Placing a plastic flyer touting the services of a computer expert was something Ethan had come up with. If the thieves drove by and found it handing on the doorknob, undisturbed, they knew they were safe to go in.

"What kind of a flyer?" she asked.

This was what she was asking about? He thought it rather odd—unless there was more to this than she was letting on.

Shrugging, Bryce said, "Just an average flyer. It was coated in plastic I guess. How the hell should I know?" And then he slanted a look at her, more convinced than ever that there was more to this. Scottie didn't talk just to hear herself talk.

"Why?" he asked. "Is it important?"

There was no point in trying to pretend that it wasn't, Scottie thought. Not after her reaction. She used to be better at masking her emotions. Now she was becoming unglued.

"It might be," she answered vaguely.

"C'mon, you don't bolt upright like that when you hear me say that there was a flyer hanging on the doorknob because it's nothing. Now, level with me, Scottie. What does that flyer have to do with all these break-ins? How does it tie in?"

She paused for a long moment, debating just how much to say, how much to leave out.

"Remember when I said yesterday that you could tell me anything?" Bryce asked.

"Yes?" she answered warily.

"Well, I think I'm going to have to insist on it right after we talk to the victims and take down their statements," he told her.

She tried to stall until she could work through this whole thing and decide just what she could tell him and what she couldn't. "I already said that after I check a few things out, I'll tell you," she reminded him.

She was hedging and he knew it. "Okay, but just remember, I can't help you if you don't help me and I really do want to help you, Scottie."

Not half as much as I want to help Ethan, Scottie thought. But she knew he was right.

"Okay," she said quietly. "After we take down the statements," she repeated, "*then* we'll have that conversation you seem so intent on having."

"It's for everyone's own good, Scottie," he told her. *"Everyone's."*

She only wished he was right.

Chapter 14

The latest break-in victims, Jacob and Mandy Williams, a fifty-ish couple, both appeared to be rather shaken when she and Bryce arrived to take their statements. As they walked up to the stylish house, it seemed to Scottie that every single light was on in the house.

"My guess is that they're probably trying to feel safe and on top of the situation," Bryce commented, noticing the look on his partner's face.

"Good luck with that," Scottie murmured. She was trying not to be overly obvious as she scanned the immediate area. She was both searching for, and hoping not to find, any sign of a trail of blood on the ground.

"You looking for something?" Bryce asked her just before they walked into the two-story house.

"Clues," was all she said.

"Crime scene unit's already here," he reminded her.

"Yes, I know," she responded, wondering if the unit, headed by Sean Cavanaugh, had found anything incriminating.

She let Bryce handle the introductions as they met with the victims, using the time to get herself under control. Her partner was savvy and she knew he'd pick up on the fact that she was acting freaked out in any manner. That wasn't going to do her, Ethan or the Williamses any good.

Hold it together, Scottie. Hold it together. She silently repeated the order like a mantra while she offered the couple a sympathetic smile.

As if on cue, she held up her identification when Bryce said her name, then waited until he paused before asking the question that was foremost on her mind.

"And you think you shot one of the thieves?" she asked Jacob Williams.

Bryce looked at her sharply, but she ignored him. Her attention was totally focused on Jacob Williams, waiting for his answer.

Williams, only slightly taller than the woman asking the question, nodded. "Well, I shot at him and the thief made a noise. So, yeah, I think I hit the dirty scum."

Her pulse accelerated but she kept her voice steady. "Where were you standing at the time?"

"Here. In the house. I don't know," Williams snapped, sounding progressively more irritated as he spoke. "When Mandy and I came in, I saw these people trying to get out the back patio door. I grabbed my gun out of the drawer in the living room desk and I aimed it at them. I yelled 'Stop.' They didn't. So I shot at the closest one. One of your people took my gun," he complained.

"Standard procedure, sir," Bryce assured the home owner. "You'll get it back after they finish processing it."

Maybe Williams had missed when he shot at the thieves, Scottie thought, praying she was right as she tried to be inconspicuous, looking at the floor. "Do you know what they took?"

Williams shook his head. "We haven't had time to look," he answered, including his wife in the answer, "but I didn't see them carrying anything."

Scottie watched as Mandy Williams threaded her hand through her husband's in mute support. Both had really been shaken up, she thought again, not that she could blame them.

"You said 'them.' How many thieves did you see?" Her question was addressed to both of the victims.

"Two—no, three," Williams corrected himself. He glanced toward his wife for confirmation. Mandy Williams nodded her head.

Scottie's heart was in her throat as she asked, "Could you recognize them if you saw them again?"

Williams was clearly frustrated. "No, it was dark. All I can say is that one of them was a large, husky man."

"I think one of them was a woman," Williams's wife volunteered. "Either that, or it was a man with a really great shape."

She glanced from Williams to his wife. "And you're sure that you didn't get a good look at any of them?" Scottie pressed.

Williams looked as if a lightbulb had suddenly gone off over his head. "No, but I've got motion-activated cameras mounted by the front door and over the patio. They have to be on that. You're welcome to look at the footage," he told them.

Bryce nodded. "Thanks, we'll have our techs at the crime scene lab take a look at them, see if they can make out any images."

Knowing the way Ethan operated, Scottie was fairly certain her brother had disabled any cameras on the premises before the thieves ever got there, but she kept that to herself.

"When you were giving your statement to the police officer, you said something about the flyer on your front doorknob not being disturbed," Scottie reminded Williams. Mentally she crossed her fingers. "You didn't throw it out, did you?"

"No, it's right here," Williams told her, crossing the room to where he had tossed the flyer when he and his wife had entered the house.

He was about to pick it up but Scottie got to it

ahead of him. Politely edging him out of the way, she used a handkerchief to pick up the flyer.

"Is it important?" Williams asked her uncertainly.

"Everything's important in this kind of an investigation," Scottie told the victim, deliberately keeping her answer vague.

Glancing at it, her heart froze. She was right. The flyer was for a computer tech.

Ethan was involved.

"Well, I think we've got everything we need," Bryce told the couple after he had asked them several more questions. Taking his card out of his wallet, he handed it to Williams. "Here's my card with both my cell phone and my number at the precinct. Give me a call as soon as you look through your things— even if you find that nothing was taken," he added.

Williams nodded, closing his hand over the card. "I'll do that." He exchanged glances with his wife. "I don't expect either one of us to get any sleep tonight, anyway. Is it okay if I call you early in the morning?" he asked.

"Absolutely," Bryce told him. "Anytime. One way or another, we'll be in touch again," he promised. Looking at Scottie, he indicated that he was ready to go unless she had something else she wanted to ask.

Scottie was more than ready to leave. Still holding the flyer with her handkerchief, she fell into step beside him. Bryce was examining the flyer and she assumed he was trying to figure out why she was holding it the way she was.

"You think the perp's fingerprints are on it?" he asked her once they had left the house.

"There's an outside chance there might be," she told him.

He caught the inflection in her voice. "You say that as if you don't think there are. The way you talked about it, I got the impression that you think one of the thieves hung this on the doorknob."

"Yes, I do." She knew he was waiting for more. Resigned, she gave him another morsel. "Wearing gloves." She hadn't expected him to react the way he did.

"You know something."

She weighed her options. Lying was only going to get her in trouble, and she needed him on her side— for Ethan if not for herself.

"Possibly," she said to qualify her response. "I want to show this to the other victims, see if any of them remembers seeing it hung on their door-knobs." She saw the impatience in his eyes. He'd humored her up until now, she needed a little more slack. "Look, this is a long shot and I don't want to say anything until I have more information. Please," she added.

This was important to her, Bryce thought. And personal. He didn't like being kept in the dark, but he also knew what it meant to be following a hunch—if that was what she was doing.

"Okay," Bryce finally agreed. "But you and I are having a heart-to-heart by the end of the day—and your part had better be good," he warned.

That all depends on your definition of good, Scottie thought uneasily.

Offering him a barely slight smile, she said, "Thank you."

He didn't want her thanking him, he wanted her being honest with him. "We'll see," he answered.

One by one he and Scottie made the rounds, going to all the other victims. Scottie showed each of them the flyer, now safely sealed in a plastic bag.

Each of the break-in victims recalled seeing a flyer hanging on the doorknob when they returned home, although a couple of them weren't sure if it had been like the one they were being shown.

Scottie grew progressively quieter with each identification. That fact wasn't lost on Bryce.

"Now are you going to tell me what this is all about?" he asked after they had seen their last break-in victims and were driving back to the precinct.

It was Sunday so the crime lab itself was technically closed, but because of the latest break-in, there was a full team presently there, examining the latest batch of potential clues that had been bagged and tagged. Bryce wanted to drop off the surveillance cameras as well as the flyer.

Most of all, he wanted answers and he felt that he had been patient long enough.

"Well?" he persisted. When she didn't say anything, he pulled over to the side of the road and turned off the engine. "I'm waiting, Scottie."

Scottie knew that she had run out of options and ways to stall. And at this point she was ready to admit that she needed help in locating her brother, no matter what kind of situation—good or bad—he had gotten himself into. She had a feeling that the people he had thrown his lot in with were definitely dangerous.

Taking a breath, she said, "I think I might know who one of the thieves is."

"'*Might* know'?" Bryce repeated. "And just how's that possible?"

She looked down at the sealed flyer she had on her lap. "Because of the MO that was used."

"The flyer?" he guessed uncertainly.

"The flyer," she confirmed.

"Okay," he said gamely. "Walk me through this. Exactly how does it work?"

Every word cost her, but she'd rather see her brother in prison than possibly dead and, if she was right, the people he was mixed up with would eliminate him in a heartbeat if something went wrong.

"Flyers get distributed throughout the neighborhood, including the potential target's house. The thieves drive by later in the day or evening. If the flyer hasn't been moved—they make their move."

"Sounds like a pretty haphazard way to operate," he speculated.

"Not if you've hacked into the target's cell phones and their emails so you can track their activities. That's how they knew that the Williamses would be out of town for three days—or were supposed to be," she amended. "Same thing for the others."

It was beginning to sound more plausible, Bryce thought. "You said you thought you might know who was pulling off these break-ins." His eyes met hers. "I assume you have a name."

Damn it, Ethan, why did you put me in this spot? Scottie set her jaw grimly. "Yes, I do."

"And that is?"

"It might not be him," Scottie told her partner, hedging. "It's his MO—or was, once upon a time," she admitted. "But it could be someone else. I mean, coincidences do happen."

He was trying his best to be understanding, but his patience was quickly growing thin. "Scottie, you're stalling."

She sighed. "That obvious, huh?"

"Yes, it is," he answered solemnly. "A better question is *why* are you stalling?" He looked at her. They were just getting to the point where he felt comfortable working with her, but not if she was lying to him. "Who are you protecting? A former lover?"

Scottie's eyes widened and she almost choked. "No. Oh, Lord, no."

"Then who? Who do you know who hung those flyers on potential victims' doorknobs and then hacked into their cell phones and their emails?"

"It's the other way around. First he hacked, then he made up the flyers to hang on doorknobs." She knew she was grasping at straws, but she wanted

Bryce to have a clear picture of the way the jobs were pulled off.

"He *made* those flyers?" Bryce questioned.

"Actually, before all that, he hacked into insurance company databases to find the names of people who had coin collections they were insuring."

The pieces were beginning to fall together and make sense, Bryce thought. "This is turning out to be rather complex, but you still haven't answered my question," he told her pointedly.

He paused to give her the opportunity to volunteer a name. When she didn't, he asked her again, this time in a more forceful voice.

"Who is it, Scottie? Who is masterminding these break-ins?"

She sat there. Her eyes began to fill with tears, something that really annoyed her. She wasn't the kind of person who used tears to her advantage or to garner sympathy. Clearing her throat, she began to speak slowly, filling Bryce in.

"I tried reaching him, but I can't. He's not answering his phone and he's not in his apartment. He hasn't been for several weeks now."

Bryce raised his voice. "Who, Scottie? Who's not answering his phone? Who's not in his apartment? I need a name, Scottie, and I need it *now*."

She pressed her lips together and then she said, "Ethan. His name is Ethan. Ethan Loomis," she told her partner, feeling like every syllable was sticking to the roof of her mouth.

"The guy with the inhaler?" he asked, remembering where he'd heard the name before.

"Yes."

She'd answered so quietly, he'd hardly heard her.

Well, at least he had a name, Bryce thought. "And where do you know this Ethan Loomis from?"

This part was even harder for her to say because Scottie felt as if she was betraying her brother somehow. She was supposed to be able to keep him safe because of her job. Instead she was going to wind up being the reason they would be arresting Ethan—if they ever found him.

Finding him was the important part, she reminded herself.

Hoarsely she said, "He's my half brother."

Bryce stared at his partner, stunned into silence for a moment. But only a moment. A myriad of emotions ran through him.

"And just when were you going to tell me this?" he asked, his voice barely controlled.

A sad smile curved the corners of her mouth. "Ideally, probably in the second or third year of our partnership," she answered.

She saw the anger in Bryce's eyes. Rather than retreat, she found herself desperately wanting to make him understand. "Look, you come from a big family, you must know what it's like to want to protect one of your own. There's something wrong here. Ethan's a good kid, really."

"A good thief," he scoffed, at a loss as to how

to react to the information, to *her*. "Now that's an original one."

"Okay, I grant he did some bad things when he was in his teens, but he got past all that. He paid his debt in juvie and when he got out, he was a totally different person. I got him a job with a gaming company. He's been working with them for the last five years and he's stayed clean, Bryce. He hasn't gotten so much as a parking ticket in all that time."

"This is a hell of a lot more than a parking ticket," Bryce replied, his voice so deadly quiet it almost scared her.

Scottie tried again. She had to get Bryce to believe her. "I've been trying to find him and talk to him. I think—no, I *know* he's been doing this against his will. Someone's forcing him to do this."

She was in denial, Bryce thought. But he wanted to be completely fair to her, even if she hadn't been that way with him, keeping him in the dark this way. "Okay, convince me."

Scottie told him everything she knew, everything that she was clinging to in the hope that although her brother was behind the break-ins, he wasn't doing it for the money. She had a feeling he was doing it to stay alive.

"I know him, Cavanaugh. I more or less raised him. When I turned eighteen, I petitioned the court to make me his guardian to get him away from our mother who had the nurturing instincts of a shrew."

"The court sided with you?" he asked.

"Completely."

"Go on."

"Things got a little rocky for a few years, mainly because Ethan was just acting out—like I said, life with our mother wasn't exactly the kind of thing they based storybooks on. But then, after he did his stint in juvie and came out, he really wanted to turn things around. He turned his back on the people who'd gotten him in trouble. I was able to get a judge to seal his records and he started rebuilding his life. He became the kind of guy you wouldn't mind your sister dating. Really," she insisted.

"Assuming I believe you, what went wrong?" he asked.

"I don't know," she answered helplessly. "I went by his apartment and, like I said, he wasn't there, but I questioned his neighbors. I found out that Ethan had been visited by his old girlfriend, or the way his neighbor described her, 'a girl with multicolored hair.'" She kept forgetting to include things and backtracked. "She was the one who got him into trouble in the first place."

"Eva Wilkins," Bryce recalled. "And he just took up with her again?"

"No, I don't think so," Scottie said, distressed. She hated this helpless feeling. "There had to be more to it than that. She had this hulk of a brother, Rubin. Maybe they kidnapped Ethan, threatened him, told him if he didn't help them pull off these break-ins, they'd kill him. I don't know, but it had to be something like that. He wouldn't do this on his own."

She shifted in her seat to look at him. The seat belt held her back so she hit the release button.

"Look, I know I haven't been the easiest person to work with, but you have to help me find Ethan. If we find him, we can get whoever else is pulling off the break-ins. He'll tell me," she said confidently. Pausing, Scottie looked at him, searching his face, for once not in the least distracted by his looks. "You do believe me, don't you?"

Bryce regarded her in stony silence, not answering her at first.

"Don't you?" she asked again, a little more desperately this time.

Chapter 15

"Yes, I believe you," Bryce finally said. Shifting in his seat, he took out his cell phone.

Scottie hadn't thought she'd feel as relieved as she did that he didn't think she was lying, but she did. Big-time.

"Who are you calling?" she asked as she watched Bryce tap out a number on the phone's keypad.

Instead of answering her he held up his hand, indicating that he needed her to be silent. The next second, she understood why. Whoever he was calling had already picked up.

"Valri? Hi, it's your favorite brother. No, your other favorite brother. Very funny," he said patiently. "Try again. On the third try, not bad. Listen, I need a favor. Yes, I know it's Sunday, but this is really important. I need you to meet me at the computer lab. We've had another break-in and I need you to track down someone doing that magic that you do."

He was silent for a moment as he listened to his sister say something, aware that Scottie was listening to every word intently and trying to piece his conversation together.

"No, I wouldn't ask if I hadn't already exhausted every other avenue. Uh-huh. Great. Okay, I'll see you there," he told Valri. "I owe you one. All right, I owe you twenty," he said, terminating the call.

He tucked his cell back into his pocket, noting that Scottie looked like she was just about ready to burst, waiting for him to say something. "If your brother's anywhere to be found," he told her, "my sister Valri'll find him."

But Scottie wasn't so sure. She'd heard things about Bryce's youngest sister, and they were all very flattering, but she wasn't exactly a novice, either, when it came to extricating information from the internet, Scottie thought.

"I've already tried," she told Bryce as he started the car again. "It's like all trace of Ethan's vanished. I think he's erased his digital footprint and everything that could possibly link up to him."

She was doing her best not to sound as desperate as she felt, but she had a feeling she was failing at that, as well.

Bryce didn't want to start singing his sister's praises, but he was more than a little confident about her abilities. "Valri likes challenges. That's why she's so good at what she does. You mentioned an ex-girlfriend, do you happen to know her name?" he asked. "Her *real* name," he stressed.

"It really is Eva Wilkins." That had been a very dark period in Ethan's life as far as she was concerned. She'd spent a lot of time visiting him in juvie and convincing him that it was in his best interests to sever any and all ties with Eva. "If he's involved with the same people as before, I know every one of their names," she answered grimly. "They're all branded on my brain."

Sailing through a yellow light, he glanced quickly in her direction before turning back to the road. "Every one?" he questioned. "Who's 'every one'?"

"The so-called 'tech gang' Ethan hung out with when he was sixteen. The ones he *stopped* hanging out with once he was released from juvie."

"You're sure about that?" he asked her. "That he stopped hanging out with them?"

She could tell he was skeptical and she would have been the first to agree that he had reason to be. People lied all the time. But not Ethan. She would have bet her life on it.

"Ethan swore to me he was through with them, that he was grateful to get a second chance and that he wasn't about to do anything to mess that up, or put me through hell again, the way he had the first time," she told Bryce. "And, yes," she added, knowing what Bryce was about to ask next, "I believed him."

The next light turned red and he was forced to come to a stop. It gave him a moment to regard her.

"Because you felt he was telling you the truth or because you *wanted* to believe he was telling you the truth?" he asked, fully aware of the games people could play with themselves when it came to people they cared about.

Scottie never hesitated. "Because he was telling me the truth," she said firmly. "We'd grab dinner together at least a couple of times a month. I would've known if something was wrong or if he was seeing Eva again. My brother might be brilliant and a computer genius, but he has a tell."

"What kind of a tell?" Bryce asked.

"When he's not telling the truth, Ethan wrinkles his nose a lot, almost as if he was coming down with a cold." She'd come close to mentioning it to her brother, then decided not to because his being unaware of the tell was in her favor. "I asked him if he was seeing anyone special the last time we got together and he said no."

Bryce nodded, taking in the information and processing it against what they already knew. "Okay, so he didn't get a chance to lie to you."

"He didn't get a 'chance' to lie because there was nothing to lie about," she insisted adamantly. She sat a little straighter, as if that would help her drive the point she was working on home. "The more I think about it, the surer I am that Ethan's involved in this against his will—and I'm still not a hundred percent sure he *is* involved."

She couldn't have it both ways, Bryce thought in exasperation. "You just spent twenty minutes laying out his MO for me, now you're telling me that you're not sure that he's involved?"

Scottie shifted, turning her eyes upon him just as he pulled into the precinct parking lot. "I'm in hell here, Bryce."

He felt sorry for her. But it was his job to stay above all of this, to see the big picture, not the little pieces that littered the terrain. And he wasn't about to allow her to get bogged down.

"We'll find him, Scottie," he promised, "and we'll get to the bottom of this. If he is innocent, then—"

"He *is* innocent," Scottie insisted.

"Then we'll find a way to prove it. I promise you, nobody's better at their job than Valri is," he told Scottie.

And just like that, she felt her eyes welling up, felt the dampness even though she was trying as hard as she could not to allow it to happen. "Damn it," she muttered.

Had she remembered something else? he wondered. "Now what?"

"I'm crying again," Scottie complained, annoyed with herself as she used the back of her hand to wipe away the tears. "I always hated women who broke down at the worst moments."

Bryce cupped her face in his hands and wiped away the one errant tear she'd missed with his thumb. "I won't say anything if you don't," he told her softly.

She let out a ragged breath, trying to smile. "You're being too nice."

"Sorry, it's in my DNA. Nothing I can do about

it," he told her, leaning in closer as he wiped away another tear that insisted on spilling out.

The moment seemed to freeze then, embossing itself on the folds of time. Very slowly, Bryce lowered his mouth to hers. It was a kiss meant to comfort, a kiss to tell her it was all right to cry. A kiss to let her know that she wasn't alone in this, that he was there for her and would continue to be there for her.

It bordered on more.

She knew she shouldn't have let it happen or, at the very least, that she should have pulled back when it began. But once his lips touched hers, she realized she was hungrier for comfort than she thought was humanly possible.

The kiss went on longer than either of them thought it would. And then, as if a bell had gone off somewhere, signaling an end, they pulled away from one another.

Feeling almost self-conscious—something he was completely unfamiliar with, Bryce cleared his throat, mumbled, "We'd better go in," and then opened his door and got out of his car.

Scottie opened the door on her side. She hardly remembered doing so, or getting out. But she did.

Once out, she took a breath, pulling herself together.

"Are you sure your sister doesn't mind coming in on her day off?" Scottie asked, feeling that her best bet was to redirect attention away from her and what had just happened between them. It wasn't easy, especially since she could have sworn her lips were still pulsing.

"Valri might complain a little, but she really doesn't mind. She likes being able to help solve crimes. I'd say she actually thrives on it. Especially since she was the baby in the family, always getting lost in the shuffle, and this is something she shines at. Something the rest of us can't do. So, no, trust me, she doesn't mind," he assured Scottie.

Entering the building, they took the elevator to the basement where the computer lab and the Crime Scene Investigation's lab were housed, taking up the entire floor.

Valri had just gotten in when they walked into the computer lab. The young woman everyone regarded as a computer wizard flashed a smile at Scottie then nodded at Bryce.

"Okay, what is it that couldn't wait until tomorrow?" Valri asked as they drew close to her.

Bryce took out the photograph Scottie had given him and placed it on Valri's desk. "I need you to track down this guy. His name is Ethan Loomis. He's one of your people."

Valri looked at the photograph and then raised her eyes to her brother's. "And by that you mean?"

"He's a computer wizard." Glancing at Scottie, he added, "And a hacker. And he's managed to erase himself. We need you to un-erase him," he said simply, as if it was an everyday occurrence. Pausing, Bryce held out his hand to Scottie. The latter took her cue and put the list she'd just written into it. "Here's a list of like-minded people he used to hang out with. Maybe that'll help you find him." He thought he'd covered everything, but just in case he hadn't, he looked at Scottie to fill in the possible blank. "Anything else?"

She looked at Valri instead of Bryce as she answered. "He's my younger brother and I think he's in trouble. The sooner we can find him, the better chance he has of staying alive."

Valri nodded, already calling up databases and putting them up on her screen side by side by side.

"No pressure here," she commented. Then, as she began typing and scrolling, she told her brother and his partner, "Give me some time to work on this. I'll give you a call if I come up with something."

And then, as her brother and Scottie were leaving, Valri looked up and said to Scottie what she knew she would have wanted to hear in her place. "Don't worry. We'll find him."

"Thanks," Scottie told her just before they left the lab.

Going down the hall, they took the flyer and the surveillance cameras to the CSI unit for analysis, briefly stating the history associated with each.

Getting back into the elevator, Bryce pressed the button for the first floor and then looked at the woman beside him. It had been a long day.

"I don't know about you, but I could stand to get something to eat. What time is it, anyway?" He felt as if he had spent the entire day working nonstop on the break-ins.

"Sunday," Scottie responded wearily. Her nerves felt as if they'd just been peeled down to their very core like the skin of a banana.

She sounded more exhausted than he did, Bryce thought. Small wonder. "That's the day, not the time. Never mind, let's just go get something to eat before we both collapse," he told her.

"Is that an order?" she asked him. She wasn't feeling hungry. If she was feeling anything at all, it was numb. Fear and anticipation of the worst were partially responsible for the way she felt.

"Pretty much," he told her. "And since I'm the lead on this case, you have to do what I say." He was teasing her, but his expression looked serious.

Bryce led the way out of the building to the rear parking lot. Since it was Sunday and late, the parking lot was close to empty. A skeleton crew was in the station, the rest were patrolling the streets of Aurora.

"You have any preferences?" Bryce asked her, breaking the momentarily silence.

"'Preferences'?" she repeated quizzically.

"Restaurant. Food. What would you like to eat? Are you even listening to anything I'm saying?" he asked her as they got into his vehicle.

Scottie flushed a little. He was right, she wasn't listening. She was thinking. And worrying. Would she wind up regretting telling Bryce about Ethan? Would Ethan regret it?

"I'm sorry," she apologized. "I guess I'm just letting my imagination run away with me."

He needed no further explanation. She was worried about her brother. He couldn't fault her. "Well, don't. That won't do you, the investigation *or* your brother any good," he emphasized. "I told you, Valri's the best there is at what she does. She'll find your brother. There's got to be a signal, a signature, *something* she can work with. And if Valri *can't* find him, then she'll find his girlfriend."

"*Ex*-girlfriend," Scottie insisted. After Ethan had gotten out of juvie, she'd deliberately forgotten about Eva. Maybe she shouldn't have, she upbraided herself. Maybe she should have kept track of the woman—just in case.

"Right. Ex-girlfriend," Bryce corrected himself for her benefit. "Somebody will get careless and when they do, Valri will be right there to get them. Until then, all you can do is wait—and not think about it," he told her firmly.

Bryce pulled up in front of one of the more high-end fast-food places in Aurora. Going through the drive-through, he asked for two burgers with everything and two orders of fries, in separate bags.

As he went for his wallet Scottie said, "This one's on me."

He was about to protest, then decided against it. Paying for the meals allowed her to feel as if she had a little bit of control over *something*. Instead he said, "Thanks," as she handed the cashier in the window the exact amount asked for.

When Bryce pulled up in front of her house, she felt as if an eon had gone by since they'd left this morning. She needed to shake the oppressive heavi-

ness that had descended over her. She needed to be
herself again.

About to open the door on her side, she turned to
him and asked, "Do you want to come inside?" Before he could answer, Scottie said in a low voice, "I
really don't want to be alone tonight."

"Then you won't be," Bryce replied.

Getting out of the car, he carried both his bag
and hers to the front door and then waited for her to
unlock the door.

Scottie opened the messenger bag and then wound
up searching for her house keys.

"You'd think in a purse this size, they'd be easy
to find," she murmured.

Finally extricating her keys, she unlocked the
door and walked in first. Scottie turned on lights
as she went.

"I can turn on the TV," she offered. "And we can
eat in the living room."

"Dinner and a show," Bryce commented. "Sounds
good to me."

She stopped in the kitchen, getting out two beers
from the refrigerator. "You're being very agreeable
and nice again," she told him. "You don't have to be."

"My DNA, remember?" he reminded her.

"So, what, every Cavanaugh is destined for saint-
hood?" she asked as she took two plates out of her
cabinet to put under the burgers and fries.

"Hell, no," he laughed. "You obviously haven't
met my cousin Ronan. Robots are friendlier and talk
more than he does. He's more like a brooding pres-

ence than a saint." Making himself comfortable on the sectional sofa, Bryce aimed the remote control at the 42-inch screen hanging on the opposite wall, turning it on. "What do you want to watch?"

Bringing the plates over to the sofa, she sat beside him, putting the plates on the square coffee table in front of them.

"Doesn't matter. I just want it on for background noise, really." Taking her bag, she placed the burger and fries on her plate.

"I thought that was what I was for," Bryce commented wryly.

"No," she corrected, "you are here for exactly what you told me that partners were for. Having my back. In this case, believing me when I tell you that I think Ethan's innocent of wrongdoing."

"That's not exactly what we agreed was going on," he reminded her. "He's not innocent of wrongdoing. What you believe is that he's doing it against his will. There is a difference," he said pointedly.

"I don't care about any differences," Scottie insisted, her nerves frayed. "I just want to find him alive," she told Bryce, feeling a lump growing in her throat.

"I get that, Scottie," he told her quietly, slipping a comforting arm around her shoulders and, for the moment, drawing her close to him, mutely conveying things he couldn't say out loud. "I do."

Chapter 16

Scottie had always prided herself on being strong, on holding it together no matter what. Maybe it was that she was on overload, she didn't know. But, whatever the reason, something just broke inside her. Broke and spilled out, causing her to became as close to needy as she had ever been in her own eyes.

The comfort that Bryce was silently offering her, conveyed by the gentle way he'd slipped his arm around her, crumbled the wall she had erected and maintained for as long as she could remember.

Scottie found herself turning her face up to his and, before she could think it through or get herself to stop, she began kissing him. Kissing Bryce as if nothing else mattered at this moment in time except sealing their two souls together.

Kissing him as if she needed to get lost in another world, a world she was silently asking him to create for her.

For them.

Her kisses were hungry, eager, ravenous. She knew she should get hold of herself, that this wasn't the person she wanted to project to the world, but there was no room for logic here, not when she desperately needed the comfort she knew in her heart he could give her.

Just this once, she wanted to be the one on the receiving end of comfort rather than the one who was giving it.

For just a split second Bryce went with the moment. Scottie had touched off a hunger within him that he had been unaware of. A hunger that threatened to become unbridled.

Still kissing her, he pulled her onto his lap, enfolding her in his arms and giving full vent to what he was feeling. And then an echo of sanity returned, tiptoeing along the perimeter of his consciousness.

What the hell was he doing? he silently demanded. This wasn't just some beautiful woman he'd spent the day with and now wanted to make love to. This was his *partner*, a fellow detective, and he was taking advantage of her exceedingly vulnerable state.

Just what did that make him?

With immense effort, Bryce forced himself to pull his head back. He caught hold of her arms and pinned them to Scottie's sides. He saw the bewildered look in her eyes, the disoriented expression on her face, and tried quickly to reason with her. To talk her out of this. Even though he would rather things had just taken their natural course because he wanted her more than he thought was humanly possible.

"Hold it, Scottie," he warned softly. "You don't want to do this."

She didn't want to think, she just wanted to let herself go and feel. For the space of however long this lasted, she just wanted to soar above all her problems, leaving them behind as if they didn't exist. As if reality was just a word without meaning.

It took her a second to find her voice. "Yes, I do," she told him. She didn't want him pulling away from her. Not now. Not when she needed him. "Are you going to make me beg?"

That was the last thing he wanted. Bryce cupped her cheek tenderly. "I just don't want you to find that you regret this."

"I won't." Her words came out almost breathlessly. "There're a lot of other things that I do regret doing in my life, but this isn't, and won't be, one of them."

Bryce knew he was already weakening, had been weakening from the first moment they had sat together on the sectional tonight. Most likely, even before then.

"All right, as long as you're sure," he conceded, his breath touching her lips less than a heartbeat before his mouth.

From that moment on, Bryce became the aggressor. Not so fiercely that she felt oppressed, but every step of the way, he was nonetheless definitely the aggressor.

He wanted her and he wanted her to know that.

Food was completely forgotten as another sort of hunger rose up and took over.

He kissed her over and over again, his lips touching every inch of her skin, setting her on fire. Arousing her passion while making her feel cherished.

Deftly, he separated her from her blouse then her jeans. She couldn't remember if she'd wiggled out of her underwear or if he'd slipped it off her. All she was aware of was that she was nude, her body heating as it pressed urgently against his on the sectional.

Scottie felt herself growing increasingly hotter, desperately eager for the final union—and yet wanting to keep that culminating moment at bay a little longer because she wanted to savor every delicious, mind-blowing second leading up to it.

She had never allowed any of the handful of relationships in her life to become serious, to grow to that point where she actually *cared* about the other person, because she'd had responsibilities that had gotten in the way, responsibilities she hadn't been able to turn her back on. Ethan had always been her first priority.

But this was different. For the time being, Ethan had been pushed into the background. Maybe she'd just broken beneath the weight of that responsibility, maybe she'd just escaped from it for a little while. All she knew was that she had this overpowering ache to make love with Bryce.

She was vaguely aware of clawing away his clothing, questing to feel his body urgently pressed against hers.

Her mouth sealed to his, she arched against Bryce, her body speaking to his, imploring him to take her.

Now—before something stopped him.

He was going to hate himself in the morning, Bryce thought. Hell, he was going to hate himself as soon as this was over, but even so, he still couldn't stop, couldn't just do the noble thing and walk away. He was convinced she was going to really regret this no matter what she said, but all the logic in the world wouldn't have been able to make him stop.

He wanted her.

Wanted her not just with that man-woman urge he'd experienced so often. This was different. He wanted her so much, he had been willing to walk away from her if she'd given him the slightest sign that she wanted it to stop, that she knew this was a mistake.

But with her eagerly encouraging him, her body moving beneath his like a seductive siren song, urging him on, there was just no way he could be the better man and stop what was happening.

Anointing her slowly with kisses all along her body, he made his way up to her mouth, his fingers linking with hers above her head.

And then he was over her, his eyes on hers, his warm breath making her shiver with anticipation. His body arched just above hers.

"Damn, but you look beautiful," he whispered softly more to himself than to her.

And then, as she arched up against him, waiting, he entered her. Once the union was attained, he began to slowly move.

The tempo in his head increased, as did the movement of his hips, going progressively faster.

Her heart hammering wildly in her chest, Scottie matched him movement for movement, picking up speed as he did until suddenly the final moment came, snatching them both up in its arms.

Fireworks went off, echoing within both their bodies.

Bryce held her tightly against him as he absorbed the shock wave that had telegraphed through each of them simultaneously.

Slowly his breathing returned to normal. His heart rate took a little longer to level out. As did hers, he noted. The fact that he could feel her heart against him, echoing his, pleased him.

Bryce felt her body relax against his. He loathed releasing his grip on the euphoria that had wrapped itself around him. He desperately needed that euphoria.

But then a strange thing happened.

As the steely bands loosened, the uneasiness that he was fully expecting didn't come. Instead he felt oddly safe, oddly secure, and content.

He shifted, moving his weight off her and lying on his side.

And he couldn't stop watching her. "Am I crushing you?" he asked.

"No, the sofa's soft," she assured him.

Still lying on his side, he continued regarding her, with a myriad of feelings rushing through him, each jockeying for priority and leaving him in a complete quandary. This was something new and he had no idea what to do about it.

Gently, he swept her hair out of her face. "Are you okay?"

She thought Bryce was still referring to the limited space available to her on the sectional. "I said you weren't crushing me."

"No, I mean are you okay?" he asked again, enunciating each word. And then he blew out a small breath, trying to own the moment. "I mean, this wasn't the way I saw the day ending."

"Disappointed?" she asked.

She had no idea what sort of lovers Bryce was accustomed to or how she measured up against them. She was acutely aware of the fact that she wasn't what anyone would consider experienced, but then, this wasn't something she did on a regular basis.

Or hardly at all.

"'Disappointed'?" Bryce repeated, looking at her as if she'd taken leave of her senses. "That's not exactly the first word that comes to mind right now. Or the fiftieth, for that matter." He raised himself a little on his elbow as he looked down into her face. "Why in the world would you think I was disappointed?"

"I'm not…that is, I don't…" Suddenly words

weren't coming. "Are you going to make me say this?" she asked, doubts flooding her.

He smiled at her, trying to encourage her to talk to him. To confide in him. Not about her brother, but about herself and how she felt. Because somewhere along the line tonight, Scottie and what she was feeling had become very important to him.

"I am if you want me to understand what you're talking about," Bryce told her.

She took a breath and gave it a try. "I don't do this very often...or maybe at all... I can't remember the last time that...well, that..."

She was obviously really struggling and he decided to put her out of her misery. Because right now she and the moment had become very special to him and really needed no explanation, long or short.

He moved the same wisp of hair out of her face. "Scottie?"

"Yes?" she all but snapped in frustration.

"Shut up."

The instruction came just before he kissed her to make sure she wouldn't continue uttering words that made no sense to him, in or out of context. He got the impression that because she had initially started out as the aggressor, she was embarrassed about the way things had evolved, while he couldn't have been more pleased or content.

He'd felt the attraction between them almost from the very first moment he laid eyes on her and he had deliberately placed that on the back burner, to see if it would simmer into something with substance or just boil away to nothingness.

He was glad it was the former and happier than he would have ever predicted that he was the one she had turned to when she'd needed someone to comfort her and to give her strength.

Although his love life had never been wanting, Bryce couldn't remember ever making love more than once in an evening.

Once had always been enough.

But something about this woman, something that went far beyond the realm of ordinary, of usual, "spoke" to an inner being within him. Scottie made him want things, relish things. It made him want to please her more than he usually strived to do in his quest for mutual pleasure.

So he made love with her again, taking delight in scaling the same heights, attaining the same wild and exhilarating ride to a place that was so familiar and yet so different each and every time they breached the gate together.

This time when the final climax came and he was able to gather together enough energy to move his body from hers, Bryce whispered against her ear.

"Next time has to be in your bed, or I'm going to wind up falling on the floor."

He didn't expect Scottie to laugh.

She didn't expect to have him make her laugh. She discovered that doing so was almost as great a relief to her as making love with him had been.

When she finally made herself stop, she sighed, the sound all but encompassing them where they lay.

"Thank you," she told him gratefully. "I didn't think I'd ever be able to laugh again."

"You will," he told her softly, gathering her in his arms again and just holding her against him. "No matter what happens, you will. And I'll be right there with you, to make you laugh. Or whatever," he added, a mischievous look in his eyes.

Scottie struggled into an upright position, her back still against the sectional, the rest of her pressed almost provocatively against his body. She saw the look in his eyes as they drifted over the length of her. Any feeling of self-consciousness that she thought would be there wasn't, which also surprised her.

But then, this had been an evening of surprises, beginning with the fact that she had trusted him enough to open up about her brother the way she had. No one in Homicide, her old department, even knew that she *had* a brother, let alone one with a sealed juvenile record. They didn't know anything about her background and that was the way she liked it.

So why did she feel so good about sharing something with Bryce that she had heretofore guarded so zealously?

It was much too late in the evening for Twenty Questions, she told herself. Too late for soul-searching, as well. As far as she knew, her soul had gotten lost somewhere between the first and second time they had made love together.

She tried, rather unsuccessfully, to sit up.

"Going somewhere?" he asked her, amused.

"I will if you move," she told him.

"Oh, right." He shifted so that she was able to get off the sectional.

Once her path was clear, she told him, "I'm going to bed."

Scottie gathered her clothes together, holding them loosely against her.

As she began to walk out of the room, she looked at Bryce over her shoulder. He hadn't moved.

"Are you coming?" she asked.

"Do you want me to come?" he asked, sounding a little surprised by the invitation. He'd taken her getting up and leaving the room as his cue to go home.

She glanced down at the clothes she was holding. "I'm not exactly in the position to hand you an engraved invitation, but, yes, I want you to come upstairs with me to my bedroom. You mentioned that, remember?" she asked, a smile bordering on wicked playing on her lips.

That was all he needed.

Grabbing up his own clothing from the floor, he hurried to the staircase and positioned himself right behind her.

"The staircase is wide enough for both of us," she pointed out.

"I know," he answered. "But to be honest, I kind of like the view from where I am."

Scottie didn't think it was possible, after having made love twice with the man, but his words created a warm wave that washed right over her body, making it tingle from her toes on up in renewed anticipation.

She didn't want to try to analyze it or to take it apart, but whatever it was—for however long it lasted—it felt absolutely wonderful.

As did she.

Chapter Twelve

Chapter 17

When she opened her eyes the next morning she
fully expected Bryce to be gone. She'd already made
her peace with that when she'd drifted off to sleep
a few hours ago.

But Bryce wasn't gone. He was right there beside
her, awake and propped up on his elbow, watching
her.

"You're still here," she murmured, wondering
what was going through his head right now. After
what had amounted to a full-scale workout she'd had
last night, she had no doubts that she probably looked
as if she'd combed her hair with an eggbeater.

Bryce couldn't tell if that was surprise or discom-
fort in her voice. "Did you want me gone?"

"No." And as she said it, she knew it was true.

She also realized that maybe she was being a little too truthful, given the situation. "But I thought you would be. We had a really great evening, but this is morning now."

Bryce laughed. "And she tells time, too." There was a fond look on his face as he said, "There's no end to your talents, is there?"

Scottie sighed, pulling the bedsheet closer to her. "You've got a love-'em-and-leave-'em reputation," she reminded him. Until this very moment, that hadn't meant anything to her one way or another. But it did now.

"No more than my brothers did," Bryce told her. "And eventually, once they found the right woman, they did all settle down." The conversation was going in a direction he didn't want to explore just yet so he dropped it. "C'mon, it's time to go to work." And then he grinned wickedly. "You'd better get a move on before I decide that maybe I should take a personal day—and make you take one with me."

"I'm up, I'm up," she declared, swinging her legs out of the bed. As she stood, she was careful to wrap the sheet around her.

Scottie paused only long enough to grab her clothes.

Making her way into the bathroom, she took what could have possibly been clocked as the fastest shower on record.

Dressed and out in under seven minutes, she announced, "The shower's all yours."

Bryce had only had enough time to get his bearings. He hadn't even picked up his clothing from the floor yet. "Damn, you're going to have to show me how you do that sometime," he told her, clearly impressed by her speed. His sisters were quick, but in comparison to Scottie, they all moved at a snail's pace.

"It's called moving fast," she said matter-of-factly. "I can make breakfast to go," she told him as he went into the bathroom.

"Like I said, you definitely have hidden talents," Bryce commented appreciatively just before he closed the bathroom door.

Fifteen minutes later, his hair still damp, he came down the stairs following the enticing smell of hot coffee and freshly prepared breakfast. He found Scottie in the kitchen, packing up what she'd just finished preparing.

"What *is* that great smell?" he asked.

"Well, I'd love to say 'me,' but I think you're referring to the English muffins with ham, cheddar cheese and fried egg I just finished making. This one's yours," she told him, pushing a brown bag toward him. "Coffee's in a travel mug," she added, nodding at the counter beside the coffeemaker.

Opening the brown bag, Bryce took a deep, appreciative whiff of the wrapped-up English muffin. He could feel his mouth watering. "I think I'm in love."

Scottie glanced up at him sharply.

Realizing what he'd just said out loud, Bryce cleared his throat, fully aware that he needed to walk that back. "I mean—"

In the true spirit of partnership, Scottie came to his rescue. "Let's go and see if your sister's made any headway with the list of people I gave her," she proposed quickly, pretending she hadn't heard what he'd just said. She didn't want to embarrass him, or herself, and that would be the end result if he attempted to correct himself in any way.

"She said she'd call if she found anything," he reminded Scottie, knowing his partner would be disappointed if there'd been no results yet.

Scottie shrugged carelessly. "I can dream, can't I?" she asked, walking out of the house in front of him.

"I believe that's one of our inalienable rights," he told her, following her out.

They arrived at the precinct in what amounted to record time. There seemed to be little traffic on the road, given the hour and that it was a Monday.

The moment he was out of his car, Bryce began to unwrap the breakfast muffin that had been driving him crazy with its tempting aroma the whole drive to the precinct.

By the time they walked up the steps to the building's rear entrance, Bryce had managed to finish half of it.

"You know, you might actually enjoy it more if you didn't wolf it down," Scottie pointed out, amazed at how fast he could put it away.

"This *is* me enjoying my food," he told her. He

grinned at her, indicating what was still left in the wrapper. "This is really good."

It wasn't often she got compliments, so rather than brush it off, she said, "Thank you."

Bryce held the door open for her, letting her go in first. "I didn't know you knew how to cook."

That had been a no-brainer. "I didn't exactly have a choice in the matter. My mother was usually passed out in the morning and Ethan needed to eat."

From her dismissive tone, it was obvious to him that she didn't want to talk about it. Stopping at the elevator, Scottie pressed the down button. "Do you think there's a chance that your sister just forgot to text you that she found something yesterday?"

"It's possible," he admitted, stretching the word. "But not likely."

They stopped at the computer lab to see Valri first. "I brought you breakfast," Scottie announced, turning over the contents of her brown bag to Valri. Bryce looked on in surprise. He'd thought she'd brought the second brown bag for herself.

Valri paused and pulled the bag over. "Smells good," she told Scottie.

"Tastes even better," Bryce told her, adding his voice to the conversation.

"She got you breakfast, too?" Valri asked, looking at her brother.

"Not 'got,' made," Bryce corrected. And then, to lighten a possible serious moment, he said, "I think my partner hopes that if she bribes you, you'll find those people on the list faster."

The look on Valri's face was not that of a woman who had achieved her goal. "I'm afraid the only thing I can tell you is that whoever this mastermind behind the break-ins is, he's managed to make himself and the rest of these people on the list disappear. I don't think these are even their real names," she added.

He'd never seen his sister this dejected. "You're telling me you can't find them?" Bryce asked.

Valri sighed, clearly frustrated with herself. "That's what I'm telling you."

He tried to kid her out of the funk she was slipping into. "Valri, I can handle there not being a real Santa Claus, but I always believed in you."

She glared at her brother, obviously at a loss as to what to tell him.

"Bryce, don't do this," she implored. When he continued to look at her, Valri sighed. "Okay, maybe there're a couple of things I can still try, but no promises," she stressed.

Bryce kissed the top of his sister's head. "You're the best, Valri. You'll come through. Enjoy your breakfast," he urged. It was his way of telling her to take a break. "Meanwhile, Scottie and I are going to go through all the files again and see if maybe we missed something that might help."

"We didn't," Scottie told him as they walked out of the computer lab. "I went all through those files with a fine-tooth comb already and we went back to talk to the victims. Nothing new is going to suddenly stand out," she told Bryce, trying not to sound as exasperated as she felt.

There was always more than one way to look at something, Bryce thought. His grandfather had taught him that. "Maybe it will if we go over it from another angle," he told her.

They started at the beginning, going over the written statements of each of the break-in victims. The statements all appeared to be almost identical in nature. The victims would return home and at first none of them would notice that anything was out of place. Their security systems were set and there were no open doors, no broken windows, nothing to indicate that anyone had been in the house during the time they had been gone. Discovery that they'd been robbed came in different forms.

In one instance, the home owner went to put away her jewelry and found the lockbox where she kept everything was empty. Her jewelry and their extensive coin collection were gone.

In another case, on a whim, the owner wanted to look over his coin collection, a ritual he liked to perform once a month. Had he not done that, there was no telling when the missing collection and jewelry might have been noticed.

In all the cases, there was more than adequate insurance to cover the losses. There was nothing, however, to help the victims get over the feeling of being violated and the feeling that they were no longer safe in their own homes.

"Each of these people changed security systems,"

Bryce volunteered, adding that to the list of things they were attempting to compare about the break-ins.

Scottie frowned, shaking her head. "Won't do them any good," she predicted. "Their systems are being hacked into so that the thieves can enter the house without a problem."

A thought occurred to him, not for the first time. "Do you think someone from the security company is behind this?"

She would have liked that. It would have been an easy solution, and it wouldn't have involved her brother. But she had to shake her head. "No. We've already noted that there are several different security companies used. That would involve too many people."

"Can your brother hack into these systems?" he asked her point-blank.

Scottie wanted to say no, but she couldn't. There really was no limit to what Ethan could do. She knew that firsthand.

So, with the greatest reluctance, she told Bryce, "Yes."

He appreciated her honesty. He knew what this had to be costing her. "You know this is not looking very good for him, Scottie."

"I don't care how it 'looks,'" she retorted. "I *know* Ethan. He wouldn't do this. Maybe he would have, years ago," she allowed, "but he worked too hard in turning his life around. *I* worked too hard helping him turn his life around. He just wouldn't do this to either of us." She searched Bryce's face, all but begging for his understanding. "You've got to believe me."

He sighed. The moment seemed to draw itself out until it was thinner than a thread. And then he sighed again, telling her, "I do. In the meantime, we keep looking for him. You've tried all his old haunts?" he asked.

"He doesn't have that many. And I tried every place I could think of." She rose from her desk.

"Where are you going?" he asked, instantly alert.

"To Forensics to find out if they managed to match the blood they found on the ground to anyone." The fact that it might have belonged to Ethan had been haunting her since the discovery.

"Call them. That's what we have phones for," he pointed out.

But she remained adamant. "I need to stretch my legs," she said, leaving the squad room.

When she pressed for the elevator, she could feel Bryce's presence. She didn't even need to turn around. Did he think she was going to do something to throw a monkey wrench into the investigation?

"Are you stalking me now?" she asked, turning to look at him.

"I told you I'd have your back in all this and this is part of having your back. We do everything together," he told her. "Besides, my legs could stand some stretching, too."

She wasn't sure if she bought all that, but for now there was no point in challenging him.

"Whatever," she murmured.

* * *

Sean Cavanaugh was busy running the mass spectrometer when Bryce walked into the CSI lab with Scottie. As ever, the head of the day lab's smile was warm and genuine when he greeted visitors to the lab.

"Ah, just in time," he told them.

"For…?" Bryce asked, allowing his voice to trail off as he waited to be filled in.

"That last home owner thought he winged one of the thieves," Sean said. "He did."

"Could you match the blood to someone's DNA?" Scottie asked.

She could almost feel her heart lodging itself in her throat. What if the home owner, Williams, had hit Ethan? What if her brother was somewhere this very moment, needing medical care, his wound becoming infected? What if—?

Sean shook his head. "No match in the system. Sorry," he apologized.

With conflicted feelings, Scottie took a giant step forward. "There's a sealed juvie record," she told the unit leader. "I've got the case number." Feeling her stomach tighten and wondering if she was going to really regret this, she recited the number from memory. "See if it matches that."

Sean looked at her somewhat uncertainly. "But, like you said, it's sealed, so I can't."

"I'm that person's guardian and I give you permission," she told him grimly. "Please, run the DNA."

Instead of hitting her with questions, she saw

sympathy in the older Cavanaugh's eyes. It both comforted her—and made her feel worse.

"This might take a little bit," Sean warned.

Bryce tamped down the urge to take her hand in mute comfort. "We can wait, Uncle Sean," Bryce told him.

Sean glanced from his nephew to Scottie. "Okay, give me a few minutes," he told them, disappearing into his office.

"Scottie—" Bryce began.

But she waved him into silence. She didn't want to hear any empty, comforting words. She wanted to be alone, but since she couldn't just take off, she was opting for silence.

"I don't want to talk right now."

"Okay. But whatever happens, we'll find a way to make it right," he promised her.

If only... Scottie wished.

When Sean returned several minutes later he walked back to the mass spectrometer and ran the test again. Since there was only one DNA pattern to compare to, the test went rather quickly.

Sean ran the test twice.

At the end, as the machine fell silent, he turned around to face the two detectives in the room.

Scottie could feel her nerves peeling apart. She couldn't stand the suspense and the tension a second longer. It took everything she had not to grab the older man's arm and demand an answer from him.

Instead she asked in the most controlled voice she could summon, "Well?"

Sean shook his head. "Sorry, we struck out again. No match."

She vaguely remembered grabbing Bryce's arm and squeezing hard, telegraphing her sense of tremendous relief. It was also to help her keep upright because her knees felt as if they were about to buckle.

"Don't be sorry," she told Sean in a husky whisper. "You tried. Guess we'll just have to go on looking for viable suspects. Thank you," she said, trying not to sound as cheerful as she felt.

It wasn't Ethan.

The blood didn't belong to Ethan. Whatever else was going on, her brother hadn't been shot, wasn't holed up somewhere with the possibility of gangrene looming over him. For the first time since the investigation had stepped up, Scottie felt almost giddy despite the fact that they were no closer to finding Ethan, or any of the other people she had known him to have once associated with than they had been initially.

Looking at her, Bryce could almost read her mind. "Your brother caught a break—this time," he clarified. "But sooner or later…" Bryce told her, keeping his voice low so no one else could overhear, "he's not going to be so lucky. Sooner or later—"

He didn't get a chance to finish his sentence. His cell phone began to ring.

"Maybe it's Valri," Scottie said hopefully, holding her breath as he took out his phone and answered the call.

"Cavanaugh. Right. Where again?" He suppressed a sigh. "Got it. Be right there." He terminated the call and shoved the phone back into his pocket. His eyes met Scottie's. "There's been another one."

Chapter 18

The scene of the latest break-in was a sprawling ranch-style house located on a quiet street situated on the north end of Aurora. The street trees were tall, having had more than thirty years to grow. They were in full bloom and bowed toward the trees opposite them like elegant courtiers greeting one another.

The entire scene appeared to be the epitome of tranquility and movie perfect.

It was hard to believe that a break-in had taken place here, Scottie thought, taking it all in as Bryce drove to the address he'd been given by the first responder on the scene.

Rather than park in the driveway, Bryce pulled up and parked next to the curb. "You up to this?" he paused to ask her.

She was already out of the car, eager to collect the newest pieces of information. "Try and stop me."

"My dad didn't raise any stupid kids," Bryce answered with a laugh. As they walked up to the front door, they passed what appeared to be a fully loaded 2017 Mercedes in the driveway. "You'd think that if they were going to rob the place, they'd be tempted to take something like this," he said, indicating the gleaming black vehicle.

"Tempted, maybe, but smart enough to leave it alone. This is a lot easier to track down than what they usually take," Scottie told him as they approached the front door.

"You have a point," he agreed, taking one last wistful look at the vehicle before Scottie rang the doorbell.

The officer who'd called Bryce opened the door to let them in.

"What'd they get?" Bryce asked the officer, walking into the house.

"Husband's prized Standing Liberty coin collection," the officer answered. "And a few pieces of the wife's jewelry. She's really broken up about it," he added quietly.

"Thanks," Bryce told the officer. "We'll take it from here." Walking into the living room, he took out his ID and held it up for the two people in the living room. Both appeared to be a little shell-shocked, especially the wife. "Detectives Cavanaugh and Scott," Bryce said, letting the couple look at his ID and then putting it away again. "Why don't you tell us everything that happened right from the beginning?"

"I'm not sure what happened," the victim, Harry Vickers, snapped irritably. "Regina and I came home from a cruise and everything looked just the way it did when we'd left it," he told them with a bewildered shrug.

"So when did you realize that you'd been robbed?" Scottie asked. In response to her question, the man's wife began to softly sob. "Take your time, ma'am," she urged the woman compassionately.

Impatient to get this over with, her husband took over the narrative. "We realized we were robbed when Regina went to check on her jewelry."

"Check on it?" Scottie queried, not sure what the man was trying to tell her.

"My father gave me this little diamond cross," Regina explained in a choked voice. She was obviously struggling to sound coherent. "It was my mother's. I never took it off, but I was afraid I might lose it on the cruise, so I left it here with some other pieces—pieces I don't wear," she added as an afterthought. "I should have taken it with me," she lamented woefully. She sounded more distressed than her husband was about his stolen coin collection.

"You had no way of knowing this would happen, ma'am," Scottie said, trying to make the woman feel a little better.

Regina Vickers's deep brown eyes filled with tears. "That doesn't change the fact that the necklace is gone," she sobbed.

"Anything else taken?" Bryce asked, trying to move the investigation along.

"Isn't that enough?" Vickers snapped then instantly apologized. "Sorry, you just don't expect something like this to happen to you. They wiped out my coin collection. I've been building it for years," he told them. "I have pictures and detailed receipts from when I purchased each piece," Vickers added.

"That'll be very helpful," Bryce agreed. "And they didn't take anything else?" he asked, already knowing the answer but wanting to be sure.

"Isn't that enough for you?" Vickers demanded.

"Just trying to get everything down accurately, sir," Bryce told him.

"I know, I know," Vickers replied, irritated. "It's just that the damn security system never even went off. What point is having one if it's not going to work?" the heavyset man demanded.

"The thieves obviously found a way to hack into the system to override it," Bryce told the victim, trying to calm the man down. "You said you just got back from a cruise. How long were you gone?"

"Eight days," Vickers answered.

"And you just got back today?" Scottie asked.

"I just said that, didn't I? We got home two hours ago," Vickers specified. Digging into his pants' pocket he took out a handkerchief and pushed it into his wife's hands. "Get a grip, Regina," he said, no doubt at a loss as to how to comfort the woman. "I'll buy you another diamond cross, a bigger one."

"I don't want another one," she sobbed. "I want *that* one."

Bryce glanced in Scottie's direction. She knew he was thinking the same thing she was. If the Vickers had been gone eight days, the break-in could have happened at any time, possibly before the one that had occurred at the Williamses' house. There was a great possibility that if one of the thieves had gotten shot, they wouldn't be pulling off another break-in so soon.

And if that thief had been seriously wounded and the members had gone into hiding, they would be that much harder to track down.

So far, according to what Sean had reported, canvassing all the local hospitals and clinics for a possible walk-in, gunshot-wound victim had turned up nothing.

They asked the Vickers a few more questions and then, handing them a card and asking them to call if anything else occurred to either of them, Bryce and Scottie started to take their leave.

Vickers walked out with them.

"What are my chances on getting my coin collection back?" he asked. "It's fully insured, so I won't be losing any money in the long run. But some of those pieces took me years to track down. They're irreplaceable."

"Kind of like your wife's diamond cross," Scottie pointed out.

Vickers appeared annoyed and somewhat embarrassed. "Yes, I suppose so."

As they walked past the Mercedes, Bryce couldn't help asking one more question. "How do you like your Mercedes?"

Vickers looked at it as if he'd forgotten it was even there. "I haven't had that much of a chance to drive it. Almost right off the bat, I had to take it into the shop. Damn thing has a mind of its own. I'm not sure I'd recommend getting one," he said honestly.

Bryce paused by the car. "How so?"

"Well, it totally shut down when I was driving to my office about a month ago. The doors all locked themselves and then everything just died. Had to have it towed to one of those high-end repair shops. There still aren't that many places that fix these things because of all the special electronics it has," he told Bryce.

"Have you had any more trouble with it since?" Scottie asked.

"No, as a matter of fact, I haven't. We drove back from the cruise in it, but I have to admit I was a little leery about driving it," Vickers confessed. "Handled like a dream, but it's like when you catch someone in a lie, you know? It takes a lot to rebuild that faith you once had."

"I know exactly what you mean," Scottie told the home owner. "Thanks for your time. We'll be in touch," she promised.

"What are you thinking?" Bryce asked as they got back into his car.

Lost in thought, Scottie blinked as she looked at him. "What do you mean?"

"I mean I could almost see those wheels in your head turning. Something's got you going," he told her, starting up his car. They pulled away from the curb and proceeded to drive out of the development. "Out with it."

"I noticed one of those so-called 'smart cars' in the Taylors' driveway when we went to take their statements. Why don't we go back and find out if they had any car trouble recently? And then we can find out how many of the other break-in victims owned these fully loaded new cars. I'm betting maybe all of them."

He heard the excitement building in her voice. "What are you getting at?"

She knew her idea was far-fetched, but in this internet age, far-fetched was only a few steps away from becoming reality.

"Aside from hacking emails and texts and checking social media postings, an excellent way to find out if someone is going to be away from home is to have a tracking device attached somewhere on a car. That's something your friendly, neighborhood, specialized mechanic can easily take care of, attaching it to some remote part of the vehicle that doesn't get to see the light of day, or noticed by the driver."

She paused to let that mouthful sink in before adding what, to her, was the crowning piece. "Did you know that those new cars can be operated remotely by anyone who knows what they're doing?"

Admittedly, Bryce was only vaguely aware of the

leaps that electronics had made when it came to automobiles these days.

"That's positively diabolical," Bryce told her, digesting what she'd just told him. "You're a scary lady, Scottie."

"I'm not scary," she denied. "I just know things you don't."

He'd always been a driver who liked to feel in control of his vehicle. His first car had been a manual stick shift he'd worked on in his garage with his cousins. "Makes me long for a 1967 Camaro."

His choice surprised her. "You like those, too?" she asked.

"You better believe it. Kept trying to find one to rebuild all through high school, but never had any luck." He realized he was getting distracted. "Okay, so, let's go back and pay our break-in victims one last visit to find out how many of them own fully loaded, new, so-called 'smart cars' and if any of those had to be taken in for work."

The answer turned out to be all of them. And each of them had taken their car in for what amounted to be minor adjustments to one of two local shops. Autos of the Future Repair Shop and another repair shop simply referred to as Matthew's Car Service.

Unlike old-fashioned, hole-in-the-wall auto repair shops whose clientele was built up through word of mouth and whose very existence was a month-to-month affair, the two repair shops that serviced one or the other of the victims' vehicles were the last word in sleek, modern and state of the art. They had to be, given the sort of vehicle they were dealing with.

Once he and Scottie had gone back to all the victims, they confirmed that each had had trouble with their vehicles sometime before the break-ins occurred.

"Looks like you're onto something, Scottie," Bryce told her. "Good catch."

They took down the date of service and the name of the repair shop that did the service.

Equipped with that information, they went to talk to the shop owners and to the mechanics who had specifically worked on the cars in question.

That was when they discovered that both shops had one mechanic in common. Marty Stevens, a nondescript man who tended to fade into the woodwork, worked part-time in both shops and had done so right from the time the repair shops had opened.

"What he doesn't know about these new high-tech vehicles isn't worth knowing," Neil Gallagher, the owner of Autos of the Future Repair Shop assured them.

"I think we may have found our man," Bryce said to his partner as they approached the mechanic, who was working at Matthew's Car Service that afternoon.

Marty was sitting cross-legged on the floor beside an ivory-colored BMW he was currently "repairing."

Bryce squatted beside him. "Marty Stevens?"

Thin, wiry and barely five-five with rust-colored

hair that easily fell prey to any hint of humidity in the air, Marty didn't even look up. "Sorry. Busy. Can't look at your car if that's why you're here."

"No. We're here about a car you already looked at. As a matter of fact, several cars you've already looked at," Scottie told him.

That got the mechanic's attention and he scrambled to his feet. "You have any complaints, talk to the manager. He handles the reimbursements," he told Bryce somewhat nervously.

"We came to talk to you, Marty," Bryce told him, keeping his tone friendly. "We'd like you to come down to the precinct with us and answer a few questions."

"I can't," the mechanic protested. "I'm busy."

"Oh, I think you can," Bryce told him. "Now, you can come voluntarily or we can place you under arrest, the choice is yours."

Marty seemed instantly skittish. Weighing his options for a moment he said, "I'll come with you."

"Good choice," Scottie told him.

They escorted the mechanic out of the shop.

"Hey, he's not finished yet," the owner protested as he saw them leave with Stevens.

"Oh, I think he might be." Bryce tossed the comment over his shoulder as they left.

"Something you'd like to get off your chest?" Bryce asked once Stevens had been brought into the interrogation room.

The mechanic appeared to shrink into his chair as

he looked from one detective to the other. He rubbed his palms on the table, leaving wet streaks. "Yeah, I don't like being questioned."

"Because you did something wrong?" Bryce asked, moving his chair closer to the mechanic's.

"Because you act like I did something wrong." Perspiration was forming on Marty's upper lip. "I didn't overcharge that guy," he protested. "That's what the owner does. All the electronics in these new cars are tricky. You have to baby them, otherwise they go haywire."

"'Haywire,'" Bryce repeated, still sounding friendly. "Is that a technical term?" he asked.

Stevens swallowed. His Adam's apple seemed to dance up and down. "Do I need a lawyer?" he asked.

"I don't know," Bryce responded, "do you?"

Scottie took her turn, doing her best to sound friendly when what she wanted to do was to grab the mousey-looking mechanic by his shirt and shake him. "Look, Marty, we're not looking at you for price gouging or for padding the final bill. That's not what we do here. We just think it's rather odd that all the vehicles you were asked to repair had tracking devices on them."

The mechanic continued perspiring, his coveralls clearly sticking to him. "Yeah, in the dashboard. It's a standard feature," Marty said nervously, staring down at the table as he shifted in his seat.

"In the dashboard, yes," Scottie agreed. "But that's not the tracking device we're interested in.

The last one we found was in the wheel well. That's *not* a standard feature," she pointed out quietly.

"There was a tracking device in the wheel well?" Stevens asked, doing his best to sound surprised. Belatedly, he raised his eyebrows.

"That's pretty bad acting, Marty," Bryce commented. "Want to give it another go?"

There was a note of building hysteria in the mechanic's voice. "I don't know what you're talking about."

"I'm talking about ten to twenty most likely—for each break-in," Bryce informed him calmly. "More if the judge doesn't like your attitude."

It was obvious that the mechanic was panicking now. "Wait, what?"

"That's what breaking and entering is going for these days," Bryce told him, making up the numbers to frighten the mechanic into a confession.

Stevens was almost beside himself. "I didn't break in anywhere," he protested, looking from one detective to the other, desperate to have one of them believe him. "I just fixed cars."

"Fixed it so that your gang knew when the owners were away from their house and it was safe to break in," Scottie said. She leaned in on the mechanic's other side so that he felt as if they were closing in on him.

"I want a lawyer," Stevens cried, his voice cracking. "I have a right to a lawyer."

"Yes, you do. But you get a lawyer and we can't

help you," Scottie said, still doing her best to sound as if she was being sympathetic.

"How? How can you help me?" Stevens asked, his head almost swiveling back and forth as he looked from one detective to the other, searching for a way out of his dilemma.

Scottie laid it all out for the mechanic. "You tell us who else is in on this, who broke into those houses and where we can find them and, for our part, we'll tell the judge how helpful you were and recommend that they go easy on you," she told the nervous-looking mechanic. "You won't have to serve the full sentences."

Stevens looked torn and exceedingly frightened. "I don't know." He turned toward Scottie. "She'll kill me if she finds out I told you anything."

"She? Who's she?" Scottie pressed. Not waiting for a name, she asked Stevens, "Is it Eva?"

The moment she said the name, the mechanic's eyes widened to almost twice their size, looking almost cartoon-like. "You know her? You know Eva?" he cried. "Then you know what she's like. She's crazy. Hell, that witch's got her old boyfriend tied up in a room. She threatened to kill his family if he didn't cooperate."

Yes! She knew it. She *knew* there had to be a reason why Ethan was involved in this.

For just one blissful second she felt the rush of relief. But the very next moment Scottie forced herself not to get excited just yet. They still had to find where that worthless witch was keeping Ethan.

She pushed a yellow lined pad and a pen in front of the frightened mechanic. "If you ever want to walk outside and breathe fresh air again, Marty, you're going to write down the name of everyone who's involved in this and you're going to tell us where we can find them."

"You mean like their addresses? I don't have addresses," Marty cried.

"How do you contact them?" Bryce asked.

"I don't," Marty said. "Eva calls me, gives me instructions."

That meant that there was an incoming number on the mechanic's phone. "Okay, Marty, this time you're going to call her," Scottie said, handing the phone that had been confiscated earlier back to him. "Tell her you've thought it over and you want more money or you're going to go to the police."

Marty looked terrified. "Are you trying to get me killed?"

"No, we're trying to get a bead on where Eva is calling from." Because she had a feeling that was where her brother was being held prisoner. "You have to keep her on the phone long enough for us to do that."

Marty shook his head almost violently. "No, I can't!"

"Tell her you want a bigger cut. That the police came to the repair shop, asking questions, and if you're going to risk everything, you want more money." Scottie could see he was digging his heels in. "Think of the alternative, Marty," she told him pointedly. "I guarantee you won't like prison."

Drawing in a shaky breath, the mechanic nodded. "Okay, I'll call her."

"Atta boy, Marty. Way to be a team player," Bryce said. He already had Valri on the phone. "Valri? I need you to trace a phone. We've got a call going in to a suspect's number and we want an address." He gave her the number of the cell phone placing the call. "This is for all the marbles, Valri," he told his sister. "Great." He looked at the mechanic. "Okay, start dialing," he instructed.

"You'll protect me?" Marty asked nervously, practically begging.

"Count on it," Scottie said.

Taking a deep breath, the mechanic swiped open his phone.

Chapter 19

The mechanic's hands were visibly shaking as he tapped the "return call" directive on his phone screen. The phone on the other end rang six times. Marty was about to terminate his attempt when he froze.

Someone on the other end of the call was picking up.

"What do you want?" the female voice snapped. "I told you no more houses right now."

Marty's eyes darted back and forth between the two people on either side of him. Scottie waved her hand at the phone, directing his attention back to the person he was speaking to.

"I—I want a bigger cut," Marty blurted.

The request was met with silence at first. And

then the woman said frostily, "You'll get what we agreed to. Now don't call me again until I tell you to—"

Watching him, Scottie made a rolling motion with her hands, indicating that he needed to stretch this out, then deliberately held up her badge. Marty looked as if he was ready to come out of his skin.

"U-um," he stuttered, "the police were here, asking questions."

"What kind of questions?" the woman on the other end demanded.

"Just questions," he answered nervously. "I didn't tell them anything." The momentum in his voice built. "But you said they wouldn't catch on to me. That I was safe. If I'm going to risk everything, I—I want more money."

"Yeah, we'll talk," the woman snapped just before the call suddenly went dead.

Marty looked at Scottie, raising and lowering his shoulders haplessly. "She hung up."

"Valri, did you get it?" Bryce asked anxiously, talking into his phone.

"There wasn't enough time to pinpoint the location, but I narrowed it down to a three-block radius," Valri told him, sounding far from happy with the results. "The call was coming from somewhere between MacArthur and Adams, along Mira Loma."

Bryce tamped down his disappointment. "Better than nothing," he told his sister. "You did good, Valri."

"I could have done better," she answered, frustration echoing in her voice. "Keep me posted. I want to know how this goes."

"Will do." Ending the call, Bryce put his cell phone back into his pocket. He saw that Scottie was already on her feet, ready to rush out and search the area.

"Can I go now?" Marty asked anxiously, pushing back his chair.

Bryce put his hand on the man's shoulder, anchoring the mechanic in place before he could rise.

"You get to stay as our guest a while longer, Marty. We'll get back to you," he said. "Keep an eye on him," he told the police officer right outside the interrogation room door. "I've got to go tell Handel what's going on," he told Scottie. "We're going to need backup."

Instead of nodding, or going with him to see the lieutenant, she was already on her way out. "Good. I'll meet you there."

"No," Bryce called after her. "You'll wait for me," he ordered. But Scottie had already raced out of the squad room. "Damn it, woman, why can't you ever listen?" he demanded sharply. The urge to run after her was strong, but there was no getting away from the fact that they were going to need backup.

Biting off a curse under his breath, Bryce hurried to the lieutenant's office.

Scottie had a hunch.

It wasn't anything more than that, but the place she was thinking of fell within the area Valri had narrowed down for them as she'd triangulated the incoming cell phone signal. There was a strip mall located on the corner of MacArthur and Avocado, just beyond Adams. Scottie knew that there was a restaurant there that had changed ownership as well as its names and the kind of food that was served there over the last thirty years. She remembered now that Ethan had told her that Eva's late grandfather had owned it once and her family had lived above the restaurant.

It had been a Greek restaurant at the time, before it became a Chinese restaurant, then a restaurant that served hamburgers and fried chicken. Its last transformation had been to a homey restaurant that had specialized in barbecue ribs and buffalo wings, but eventually that had gone out of business, as well. That was its current state.

That didn't, however, change the fact that there were living quarters above the restaurant.

Scottie upbraided herself for not remembering that fact sooner.

Parking her car a full block away from the strip mall, she carefully made her way to the abandoned barbecue–buffalo wings restaurant. There was a lock attached to the front door, barring entry. Working her way around to the back of the restaurant where deliveries had once been made, she tried that door. It presented no challenge. She picked the lock she found there in seconds.

Entering, Scottie drew out her weapon, held her breath and very slowly—just in case they squeaked—

made her way up the back stairs. As she came closer to the landing, she could hear the sound of several raised voices, arguing.

"Look," a deep male voice was saying. "We've got enough. We blow this place and lay low for the next six months or so. They're not onto us yet. And if pretty boy here doesn't like our travel plans, we can leave him here. In a nice, tidy grave. He can't be the only nerd who knows how to hack security systems."

"I'm with him," another voice, deeper than the first, agreed. "We don't need deadweight. Emphasis on the word *dead*," he added with a laugh that made Scottie's blood run cold.

She wanted to go in, but held herself in check a moment longer. It was better to know how many people she was up against before she barreled in.

"This is my plan, we'll do it my way." This time the hard, raspy voice she heard belonged to a woman.

That had to be Eva, Scottie thought, which made three people in the gang. Counting Ethan, that made four. Maybe that was all there was. She recalled there were five members the first time Ethan had been caught, but maybe they could only find four this time.

"You jerks can be replaced," she heard Eva snarl. "He can't."

"I count two votes to your one," the man with the deeper voice said. "You're outvoted."

She hadn't heard Ethan say anything yet. Why? Was he the one who had been shot, after all? Was he—?

One of the men cursed and then something like

two barely audible "pops" went off. Her heart began to pound. Was that a gun? With a silencer? Who shot whom?

Afraid she'd already waited too long, she knew she couldn't just stand outside the door any longer. Her brother's life could be at stake—*if* he was even still alive.

Bryce's face flashed before her eyes a second before Scottie slammed opened the door with her shoulder. Pain radiated all through that shoulder as she focused on the lone person standing in the room.

A woman with blue, green and pink hair.

Eva.

Scottie instantly trained her gun on the woman. Only then did she see that her brother was in the room. He had duct tape over his mouth and was tied to a chair that was up against what she assumed was the computer that he used.

Her throat almost closed up. He was alive!

"Drop the gun, Eva!" she ordered.

The woman spun around on her heel. "Well, well, well, look who it is, Ethan. It's your big sister to the rescue again. She figured out where to find us. I guess you're not the only one with brains in the family."

Tall, sexy and dressed all in black, Eva Wilkins was holding a gun with a silencer on it, just as she'd surmised. Eva had her gun trained on Ethan.

"And everything was going so well, too," Eva jeered. And then her eyes narrowed. "If anyone's dropping a gun, it's going to be you, Big Sister. Drop the gun or your little brother's going to have a hole in that brilliant head of his."

"I wasn't born yesterday," Scottie told the woman. "I drop my gun and you shoot him anyway."

Eva's face darkened. "I haven't done it yet, have I? I just shot those two other jerks because they wanted to get rid of Ethan. That should tell you something."

"It tells me that you're psychotic and enjoy killing people," Scottie told her.

A nasty laugh escaped Eva's lips. "Good one. You didn't tell me that your big sister had an even bigger mouth, Ethan." Eva slanted just the slightest glance in his direction. "Oh, I forgot, you can't answer me because I gagged you. You really never did have an appealing voice anyway. But your hands, well, that's another story, isn't it? Those magic fingers of yours could just do wonders. On the computer and on me," she added.

"I really was shooting for a happily-ever-after, you know, pardon the pun," Eva added. Her voice grew hard. "Now I'm only going to tell you this one more time. Put the gun down, honey, or say goodbye to your little brother."

Eva's expression was hard as she cocked the trigger of the gun she was holding. The weapon was still aimed directly at Ethan.

Her eyes shooting daggers at the woman, Scottie slowly bent and, never taking her eyes off Eva, placed her weapon on the floor in front of her.

Eva's smile bordered on pure evil. "Just as I planned," she pronounced. "Say goodbye to your

Big Sister," Eva told Ethan as the woman aimed the weapon directly at her.

A single shot rang out.

Scottie ducked the moment Eva had told her brother to say goodbye, diving for her weapon. But she realized a heartbeat later that it wasn't necessary. Because Eva was no longer standing. She was on the floor. There was a single bullet hole dead-center in her forehead, blood oozing out of it.

Clutching her gun, Scottie scrambled to her feet and swung around, ready to shoot whoever was behind her.

"I guess that wasn't part of her plan," Bryce said, looking down at the dead woman's utterly shocked expression.

Stunned, Scottie lowered her weapon to her side. "How did you find me?" she asked. It couldn't have been just luck that had Bryce arriving on the scene just in time.

"I had Valri track the signal from your phone," he answered simply.

Squatting beside Eva, he checked to make sure she was dead, then made his way to the other two bodies on the floor. They were both dead, as well.

Scottie hurried over to her brother to take the tape off his mouth. The moment that she did, Ethan started talking. "I didn't want to help her, Scottie. I swear I didn't. But she had that ape of a brother of hers kidnap me, and then she told me if I didn't help her, she'd kill you. And I know her, Scottie. She would have done it."

Scottie couldn't begin to describe the relief she felt at finding her brother alive.

"I believe you," she told Ethan. "And what matters now is that it's over." She looked around at the three bodies on the floor. "Really over." Using her jackknife, she quickly cut through his ropes. "Do you know where she stashed the stolen goods?"

Her brother was slightly unsteady on his feet. "My legs have gone numb," he explained. He fell back into the chair that had been his prison for most of the last month. "But I overheard them talking, so I've got a pretty good idea where everything is. She gave it to Rubin to fence."

She looked at the two dead men on the floor.

"Which one's Rubin?" Bryce asked.

"That would be me." Scottie turned to see a giant of a man standing in the doorway. This had to be Eva's brother, she thought. The next second, she felt Bryce pushing her behind him to shield her.

"Looks like you went and had a party without including me," Rubin said. "That's okay. More for me," he concluded. If he was upset to see that his sister had been shot, he gave no indication.

"You might as well give up," Bryce told him, silently cursing the fact that he had holstered his weapon. "Backup will be here any moment."

"Backup? Is that the best you've got? I'll be gone by the time they get here. And they can handle the cleanup." Rubin smirked. "I don't believe in loose ends." Saying that, he swung his gun toward Ethan, aiming it at him.

Scottie screamed, "No!" and dove at the gunman just as his gun went off. Because she butted into him, Rubin's aim was thrown off.

The giant of a man emitted an animal-like cry as he crumpled, thanks to the bullet that caught him in the back of his knee. A barrage of curses followed.

Startled, both Bryce and Scott looked to find Duncan standing exactly where Rubin had been a moment ago. The gun in Duncan's hand was still smoking.

"You delivered my son, I saved someone who's obviously important to you," he told Scottie. "I'd say that makes us even." Temporarily holstering his weapon, he said, "In case you haven't figured it out yet, I'm your backup. At least until the others get here."

Bryce looked at him, confused.

"Valri called me. Your backup got caught up in a traffic jam. Something's really got to be done about the power grid in this city," he commented. "That's the second time traffic lights have gone out in a month."

"I don't know how to thank you," Scottie said, blinking back tears as she addressed the words to both Bryce and his brother. "Both of you."

"Well, I don't know about him—" Bryce nodded toward his brother "—but I've got an idea how you can thank me," he said in a voice that was low enough for only Scottie to hear.

"Let's put a pin in that for a second," she said, an amused, sexy smile playing on her lips. Turning toward her brother, she said, "You realize you're going to have to come into the precinct and give your statement."

"I will do *anything* that you and the police department want me to," Ethan said, rotating his shoulders as he tried to get feeling back into them, as well. "I just want this whole nightmare to be behind me. And first thing tomorrow, I'm going to the animal shelter and getting a big German shepherd."

Scottie looked at him, at a loss where he was going with this. "Why?"

"Because nobody's going to try to kidnap me if I answer the door with a German shepherd standing next to me, snarling."

"Is that what happened?" Bryce asked. The sound of approaching sirens cut through the air and was getting louder.

Ethan nodded. "Eva showed up at my door and said she wanted to talk. I opened the door, told her there was nothing to talk about, and the next thing I knew, I woke up here, all tied up."

"You were tied up the entire time?" Scottie questioned.

"No." He sat again, obviously still feeling weak. "I got bathroom breaks and they untied my hands when they wanted me to work on the computer, or when they gave me something to eat. But for the rest of the time, I've been a prisoner here since Eva had me kidnapped." He stopped for a moment, as if collecting his thoughts. "I did manage to convince them that it was smarter to conduct the robberies when no one was home. Otherwise, I think a lot more people would have been hurt besides Rubin." He nodded toward the man who was cursing up a storm, saying his knee was shattered. "He got shot during the last break-in, but it was just a flesh wound," Ethan added.

"I guess that ties up most of the loose ends," Bryce said. "Let's get you back to the station. The sooner we get your statement, the sooner we can wrap all this up."

Relieved beyond words that her brother was all right and that this ordeal was finally over, Scottie smiled up at her partner. "Sounds good to me," she told him, grateful that, for once, she'd let her guard down enough to share her burden with someone. Otherwise, neither she nor her brother might have lived out the day.

"Give me a minute, okay?" Ethan requested.

Scottie turned to look at him. "Something wrong?" she asked.

"No, I—" Ethan didn't finish answering her. Instead he crumpled to the floor right in front of her, unconscious.

Chapter 20

Frightened, Scottie immediately bent over her brother.

"Ethan? Ethan, talk to me," she begged, trying to rouse him while she quickly scanned his torso for any possible bullet holes she might have missed.

"Not something he can do right now," Bryce told her, squatting beside her brother. He felt for a pulse and was relieved to find one. "He's unconscious. I need two buses sent out immediately," Bryce requested when he heard a voice come on the line in response to his 9-1-1 call.

He gave the dispatcher the address then terminated his call.

"My guess is that, given what he's been through and how you found him, he's probably just really dehydrated, Scottie. You can get a better idea of what's wrong once they have him in the ER," he said, gently easing Scottie away from her brother and helping her back to her feet.

Upright again, she blew out a shaky breath. "You're right. I should focus on the fact that he's alive. I wasn't a hundred percent sure that he would be," she confessed.

"Well, he is and he's going to be fine," Bryce told her in an authoritative voice that left no room for argument or doubt.

In her heart she knew that Bryce couldn't guarantee what he'd just said to her, but she appreciated the fact that he was deliberately giving her something to hang on to, just as he had when he'd told her initially that they would find her brother. His upbringing had made him a far more positive person than she was and, right now, she needed to tap into that.

"Thank you," she told him.

Rather than say anything, Bryce just squeezed her hand. They both ignored Rubin, who was on the floor, handcuffed and cursing them both to hell.

The sound of approaching sirens grew louder. The ambulances were on their way.

Ethan still had not regained consciousness when she rode with him in the ambulance. She held his hand, a thousand fragmented memories crowded her head, reminding her of the long, hard climb she and Ethan had had, to get to a stable plateau in their lives as well as to a stable relationship with one another.

The second the ambulance doors opened, Scottie quickly jumped out and then followed her brother's gurney into the ER.

She would have followed it into the exam room if she hadn't been stopped by one of the nurses.

"I'm sorry, you're going to have to wait out here," the older woman told her, standing in her way and barring her access.

Swallowing her protest, Scottie retreated only as much as was absolutely necessary. She waited in the corridor while the physician on call was brought in to examine her brother.

She hardly remembered sitting in one of the seats against the wall.

Her imagination kept running away with her.

In an effort not to panic, she deliberately shut it down. It would do her no good to speculate and drive herself crazy with different scenarios of what might have been done to Ethan to coerce him to help plan and execute the break-ins. She knew that he had been adamant about staying out of trouble. For him to have helped Eva, a woman he'd only a few months ago described to her as "Toxic Evil," she knew he'd been given no choice.

She felt her eyes moistening. Ethan had almost gotten himself killed just to protect her. He should have known she could take care of herself.

Hadn't she always?

"What a time for you to play the hero," she murmured under her breath to the brother hidden from her behind the exam doors.

"This seat taken?"

Startled, Scottie looked up to see Bryce standing over her. She'd been so lost in the awful scenarios she was conjuring up, she hadn't even heard him approach. "What are you doing here?"

Sitting next to her, Bryce struck a nonchalant tone as he answered, "I was kind of in the neighborhood and thought I'd stop by to give my partner some moral support."

Scottie glanced at her watch. It was late. She'd completely lost track of time. "Don't you have a home to go to?"

"I can go to it later on. It'll still be there," he told her. "So, how's your brother doing?" He nodded toward the closed door. "Did the doctor come out and tell you anything yet?"

Another wave of helplessness washed over her. It was getting harder and harder for her to just rise above it and not succumb to the dark thoughts that were plaguing her.

Scottie shook her head. "Not a word. Not yet." She looked at Bryce. He'd already done so much for her. She didn't want to put him out any more. "You don't have to stay here and keep me company."

He made no move to get up. "I'm lead on this case. That means you don't get to tell me what to do." His eyes narrowed just a little as he remembered the way he'd felt when she'd taken off earlier. "It also means that you were supposed to listen to me when I told you to wait," he reminded her.

"I know. And I'm sorry. But if I had waited, they

might have killed Ethan. Besides," she told him with a grateful smile, "you did come in the nick of time."

"Almost didn't," he reminded her. He wondered if she had any idea how afraid he'd been that he wouldn't manage to get to her before something bad happened. One second later and he could have just as easily watched her being zipped up in a black body bag.

"I know, but you did," she pointed out and then said quietly, "I never thanked you for saving my life."

"No, you didn't," he agreed, his expression unreadable.

She turned her face up, her eyes meeting his. "Thank you."

"About that," he began sternly. "You run off like that again after I tell you to wait and there will be hell to pay, Detective Scott."

She didn't doubt that he meant it. "I will try to remember that."

"Don't try," he told her with controlled anger. "Remember."

Grateful as she was to him for everything—helping her locate Ethan, saving her life—she felt she had to point this out. "You would have done the same thing in my place."

He wasn't about to let her off the hook so quickly. Especially since she had scared the hell out of him. "We're not talking about me, we're talking about you," he told her.

"Excuse me, are you here about Mr. Loomis?"

The attending ER physician asked the question as he walked up behind them.

Scottie popped to her feet as if she was sitting on a spring-triggered cushion.

"Yes," she responded breathlessly, "how is he?"

"He was severely dehydrated, but we've got him on an IV to take care of that. The tox screen we did on him turned up a drug we're trying to narrow down… I think it's safe to say that wherever you found him, he didn't go there voluntarily. I'd like to keep him here overnight for observation but I don't see any reason, barring complications, that we won't be sending him home tomorrow."

"That's wonderful news, Doctor," Scottie cried, fighting back tears of relief. "Can I see him?"

"I gave him something to make him sleep. Detective Cavanaugh filled me in earlier," the doctor went on. "Your brother's been through a lot and his body needs the rest. But he'll be awake in the morning," the ER physician promised. And then he looked at her pointedly. "In the meantime, I suggest you get some sleep, too. In my considered medical opinion, you look like you haven't been getting any sleep recently, either." He paused, allowing her to fill him in if she chose.

"Long story, Doctor," Scottie told him, the corners of her mouth curving. "But now that my brother's been found and he's safe, maybe I'll finally get some sleep, too."

The physician looked at her over his glasses. "I strongly advise it."

Bryce put his arm protectively around her shoulders, silently indicating that he was taking charge. "I'll see that she does, Doc," he told the physician. He began to steer Scottie toward the exit.

"You're not the boss of me," Scottie told him, trying to keep a straight face as she said it. It was obvious that she had no intentions of fighting him on this.

"Shut up, Scottie, and keep walking," Bryce told her, then added for her benefit, "I parked the car right across from the ER entrance."

"Are we going back to the precinct?" she asked Bryce as she got into the car.

He gave her a puzzled look, wondering why she'd think that. "You heard what I said to that ER doctor. I'm taking you home."

"But we have to file our reports on the case."

"We got all the bad guys," Bryce reminded her. "The reports can wait until morning. Besides, our only witnesses are in the hospital. Your brother's asleep and, according to the text Duncan sent me, now that he's been patched up, Rubin's singing like a canary in between cursing up a blue streak. He told Duncan where to find all the stolen goods. Seems that they hadn't been fenced yet," he told her with satisfaction. "The lieutenant sent a team to retrieve everything. Case closed," he declared.

"But we could still write up most of the reports," Scottie protested.

She was exhausted, but at the same time, extremely wired. Even though she'd told the ER physician that she thought she could finally get some sleep, she highly doubted it.

At least, not immediately.

"Do you never not argue?" Bryce sighed as he shook his head. He was clearly going to have his hands full dealing with her. Somehow, he didn't mind it.

"Wait, there's too many negatives in that question for me to sort out properly and my head hurts."

He spared her a look, doing his best not to allow the smile he couldn't suppress to curve the corners of his mouth.

"Funny, mine does, too," he told her. "I just figured it was a side effect from dealing with you."

She leaned back in the passenger seat, finally allowing herself to exhale. Really exhale. It was hard to believe that this was really over—or at least that it was in the homestretch.

"What's going to happen to Ethan?" she asked.

"Well, seeing as how he was held prisoner and forced to plan and execute those break-ins against his will—and since everyone who could possibly contradict his story is dead or under arrest—I'd say nothing." Had she thought of something to change that? "Why?"

She laughed softly at herself before she answered him. "I've been worrying about him for so long, it's just hard to stop worrying, I guess."

"Well, stop," he ordered. And then he said something she wasn't expecting to hear. "No guy wants to have his big sister hovering over him as if he's some fragile, breakable kid who needs help tying his shoes."

She wasn't sure she liked the picture he was painting. "I don't do that," she protested.

Bryce didn't bother arguing the point. That would get him nowhere. Instead he built on what she'd just said. "Good, so stop trying to take care of him and give the guy a chance to take care of himself."

She was about to repeat her denial that she was trying to take care of her brother, then stopped herself. "Maybe there's a germ of truth in what you're saying."

"'Germ'?" Bryce repeated incredulously. "How about an entire infestation?" Bryce suggested.

"Don't get carried away, Cavanaugh," she told him as they pulled up into her driveway. "I owe you a lot, but that's not going to stop me from arguing with you."

"I'm fully convinced that *nothing* would ever stop you from arguing," he told her, amused.

"Oh, is that so?" she asked, getting out of Bryce's car.

"Yes, that's so. So I'm not going to argue with you. I've got something else in mind," he told her.

"Oh? Like what?" she asked.

"Well, the case is solved, your brother's alive and well and there's every reason to believe that our victims will be reunited with their 'treasures' in the not too distant future, so I'm thinking that a little victory celebration might be in order. Feel like going to Malone's?" he felt obliged to ask, although that wasn't his first choice.

She stared at him, stunned at the suggestion. "You're serious?"

He laughed then, catching her up in his arms and kissing her right in front of her front door. Drawing back, he said, "Not in the slightest. At least, not about going to Malone's."

There went her heart again. His close proximity had a habit of doing that to her. She hoped that never changed. "What are you serious about?"

Bryce took the key from her hand, unlocked her door, then gave the key back to Scottie as he pulled her into his arms again. "The celebrating part."

Scottie laced her arms around his neck. "Right out here?" she asked just before he brought his mouth down to hers and she allowed herself to fall deeply into another delicious kiss.

"No," he answered after a couple of minutes had passed and he finally drew his lips away from hers. "We don't get to the good part until we go inside," he told her.

She could feel joy dancing through her veins as she looked up at him. Everything in her world was finally in the right place and she had him to thank for that.

And she fully intended to—for as long as he would let her.

"So what are we waiting for?" she asked.

He laughed, delighted. "Not a damn thing."

And with that, Bryce pulled her inside the house and shut the door. "You're not too tired?" he asked her.

Anticipation was ramping up all through her. "What do you think?"

"I think I should shut up and find out for myself," he told her, trying—and failing—to appear solemn.

Laughter bubbled up in her throat as she told him, "Good idea."

It was the last thing either one of them said for a very long, long time.

Chapter 21

"So, are you going to put in for a transfer back to Homicide?"

Bryce had made hot, exhilarating love with her until she was at the point of elated exhaustion. From what she could determine, he wasn't exactly far from that himself.

So when he asked her if she was transferring, it was definitely *not* the sort of pillow talk she'd been expecting.

Pulling the sheet up against her, Scottie looked at the man lying beside her in bed. The full moon's rays were invading her bedroom, but not enough for her to be able to read the expression on Bryce's face. She was left to feel her way around in this brand-new territory she'd found herself in.

"Do you want me to?" she asked him.

He looked at her in surprise. "Why would you think that?" he asked.

"Why would you ask that?" she countered. "If I'm transferring back," she clarified in case that had somehow gotten lost in the exchange.

"Well, you transferred to Robbery in order to shield your brother in case he did have something to do with the break-ins, so now that we found him and he's okay—and his girlfriend and her cronies are never going to be a threat to him—or you—again— I thought that maybe you'd want to transfer back to Homicide. I mean, it's not like you initially transferred out because you wanted a change."

She was still trying to figure out what he wanted her to do. After making love with him, she thought she understood him, but now, she wasn't so sure.

"What would you like me to do?" she asked.

Her question surprised him. She wasn't behaving the way he would have thought she would.

"You're asking me?"

"Well, you are the only other person in bed here besides me, so, yes, I'm asking you," she answered, amusement in her voice.

He was honest with her. "I don't want you to transfer back. I want to be able to walk in every morning and see you sitting at the desk across from me."

She never thought she could feel so good about something so minor. "Okay, then I won't transfer back. I guess that settles that."

"Not entirely," he told her.

Her heart did a little hiccup. Was there more? "What did I forget?"

"I was thinking along the lines of a more…permanent arrangement," he told her, winding a strand of her hair around his index finger.

She had to remind herself to breathe. He couldn't be saying what she thought he was saying, could he? "What kind of a permanent arrangement?"

He let the strand of hair fall and he took a breath. "Let me back up for a second."

She was desperately trying to follow this. "You mean like someone getting a running start before they go off a diving board?"

Bryce laughed. "Not exactly what I'm going for, but that'll do for now. Your brother is a genius when it comes to doing things on the computer."

"I really wish he wasn't."

"What if we have him use his 'powers' for good?" Bryce suggested. "I know that both Valri and Brenda could use the extra help," he told her, mentioning the Chief of Ds daughter-in-law, who was the head of the computer lab. "They're both really sharp and both really overworked. Having someone else with them in the lab who was on top of his game, like your brother, would really be welcomed. Plus, as an added bonus, you get to keep an eye on him—if that's what you want," he added.

"But he's a civilian, not a cop," she reminded Bryce.

"Doesn't matter. The police department hires civilians," he told her.

That sounded too perfect. "You can make that happen?" she asked him.

Bryce grinned. "I'm a Cavanaugh. I can do anything." And then he laughed. "I can make the suggestion," he told her. "But if Ethan turns out to be half as good as you say he is, it shouldn't be hard to make the arrangements."

Overjoyed, Scottie threw her arms around his neck. "That would be absolutely wonderful," she cried.

"Let me talk to Uncle Brian and to Brenda. By the time your brother's well enough to get back to work, all the kinks should be all worked out," he told her.

Scottie looked at him knowingly. "You're doing this so I'll stop worrying about Ethan, aren't you?"

"I don't think it's in your nature to ever stop worrying about Ethan, but this'll definitely help. Besides, Valri really is overworked. Not that I'm not part of the problem," he admitted, "but this might help everyone out. You, Ethan and Val. What do you think?"

"I think I love you." Her eyes widened as she realized what she'd just blurted out. "I didn't mean that," she quickly told him, horrified.

Bryce's expression was totally unreadable. "You didn't?"

Telling a guy you loved him was a surefire way of spooking him and making him bolt. She knew that. It was just that she'd been as caught off guard by her declaration as he had to have been.

"No."

"Oh." His mouth curved with a soft smile. "Too bad. I kind of thought it sounded nice," he told her.

"It didn't freak you out?" she asked uncertainly.

"It should have," he agreed. "But, strangely enough, it didn't. It felt...right," he concluded, finding the word he wanted.

"Right?" she questioned even more uncertainly than she had a moment ago.

"Yeah." He drew her closer to him. "Like this is a brand-new avenue that should be explored."

This was definitely serious. "Maybe we shouldn't be having this conversation naked."

"Oh, this is the best way to have this conversation," he assured her.

He was making her crazy, spacing his words with small, arousing kisses all along her face, her neck and every other inviting part of her.

As she curled her body into his, meeting his kisses with kisses of her own, Scottie heard him whisper against her hair, "Want to know a secret?"

"Yes," she breathed.

"I love you, too."

Startled, she stopped mid-kiss and looked at him. He loved her. He'd just said he loved her. Her heart hammered harder every time she silently repeated the words in her head. "What do we do about this?"

"Oh, I think we'll figure out something," he promised her.

And eventually, they did.

* * * * *

Join Britain's BIGGEST Romance Book Club

50% OFF your first parcel

- **EXCLUSIVE offers** every month
- **FREE delivery direc** to your door
- **NEVER MISS a title**
- **EARN Bonus Book** points

Call Customer Services
0844 844 1358*

or visit
millsandboon.co.uk/subscriptior

* This call will cost you 7 pence per minute plus your phone company's price per minute access charge.

BKCB3

MILLS & BOON®
are delighted to support World Book Night

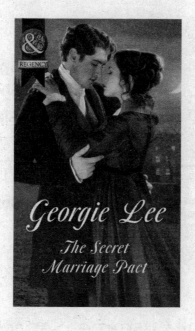

Georgie Lee

The Secret Marriage Pact